C

'The world must be full of women who would be only too eager to marry all this, Luc,' Carrie said, gesturing to the palace and the view beyond its windows.

'Oh, and you of course,' she continued cynically. 'After all, you're such a catch, aren't you? A real-life prince, with so much to offer—your arrogance, your snobbishness, your lack of any real emotional depth…'

'That's enough.' Luc stopped her coldly. 'But you are right about one thing, Carrie. It will be easy for me to find a wife. Very easy. In fact…'

The smile Luc was giving her was not a kind one, Carrie recognised, and something in his expression suddenly made her shudder, made her regret her emotional outburst of pent-up bitterness.

'In fact,' he repeated softly, 'I have already done so! *You* must marry me, Carrie…'

Penny Jordan has been writing for more than twenty years and has an outstanding record: over 150 novels published, including the phenomenally successful A PERFECT FAMILY, TO LOVE, HONOUR AND BETRAY, THE PERFECT SINNER and POWER PLAY which hit *The Sunday Times* and *New York Times* bestseller lists. Penny Jordan was born in Preston, Lancashire, and now lives in a beautiful fourteenth-century house in rural Cheshire.

Recent titles by the same author:

MARCO'S CONVENIENT WIFE
THE SHEIKH'S VIRGIN BRIDE
ONE NIGHT WITH THE SHEIKH

THE BLACKMAIL MARRIAGE

BY
PENNY JORDAN

MILLS & BOON®

First published in Great Britain 2003
Harlequin Mills & Boon Limited,
Eton House, 18-24 Paradise Road, Richmond, Surrey TW9 1SR

© Penny Jordan 2003

ISBN 0 263 83704 1

Set in Times Roman 10½ on 12 pt.
01-0104-49941

Printed and bound in Spain
by Litografia Rosés, S.A., Barcelona

PROLOGUE

'So, YOU realise now that I was telling the truth when I warned you that you could never be anything other than a momentary diversion to my godson?' The Countess gave an elegant, contemptuous shrug. 'How could it be otherwise? Luc is a prince, of noble blood and destiny. Of course he is also a man, and you are a very pretty girl, and...an available one!' Another shrug, this time a disparaging one, accompanied her coldly dismissive words, whilst Carrie's face burned with humiliation and anguish.

'It was perhaps inevitable that he should pursue you. But he will never marry you! How could he? You are nothing. Nobody! The daughter of a mere employee, that is all! A foolish and immoral young woman the whole principality knows has thrown herself at him and inveigled her way into his bed! When Luc marries it has to be to someone of appropriate background and status. The most suitable candidate to become his wife is, of course, my own granddaughter. And it is to this end that she is presently being groomed and educated.'

Carrie stared at her tormentor in shocked disbelief. She had known, of course, about the Countess's antagonism to the relationship developing between Luc and herself, but she had never dreamed that the older woman was calculatedly planning to have Luc marry her young granddaughter.

'But Maria is only ten years old, and Luc is almost twenty-five!'

The Countess gave Carrie another cold look.

'Age does not come into it, and besides, what is a mere fifteen years? My own late husband was over twenty years my senior! However, I digress. I have sent for you today, Catherine, in order that I may carry out Luc's instructions. Luc wishes you to leave S'Antander immediately. Furthermore, he does not wish to have any future contact with you.'

'No!' Carrie protested. 'No, I do not believe it.'

One thin arched eyebrow rose superciliously.

'Why? Because Luc took you to his bed? You are not so naïve, Catherine. You know how the world works beyond our borders. After all, it is only your school holidays you have spent here in S'Antander with your father and your brother.'

'But Luc—' Abruptly Carrie stopped. Luc had not made any declarations of love to her, nor given her any promises, she knew that, but she had believed that he shared her feelings, and that it was only a matter of time before he told her that he loved her as much as she did him!

Last night when he'd informed her that he was going away on business she had never imagined that anything like this could happen! And when he had insisted that she was to return to her own bed instead of staying in his, as she had so longed to do, she had thought it was because he wanted to protect her reputation. But now her wonderful, precious romantic dreams had been brought crashing down by the cold reality of his godmother's announcement.

How could Luc love her when he had instructed his godmother to treat her so ignominiously and to send her away?

Carrie admitted that up until this summer her feelings towards Luc had been slightly ambiguous. Seven years her senior, he was someone who had always taken his duties and his responsibilities seriously. He'd always held himself slightly aloof, which made her feel small and unimportant, even though she knew of the mutually high esteem that existed between Luc and her father, who had been commissioned by Luc's late guardian to advise and educate Luc on the complexities of international economics and finance. She knew too that within a matter of months the present Regency of the principality's elders, set in place to govern the country until Luc reached the age of twenty-five, would come to an end and Luc would become the principality's ruler.

'Luc what?' the Countess challenged her icily. 'It is obvious that he has now lost interest, having satisfied his sexual curiosity about you! My godson is a man of pride and principle who knows where his duty lies. All you were to him was a momentary diversion which he now wishes to forget. Surely you must realise that yourself, after hearing what he has instructed me to tell you?

'Your father tells me that you have been offered a place in his own old university college. There must be a great many things you need to do in England in preparation for beginning your degree. A seat has been booked for you on tomorrow morning's flight from Nice to Heathrow. My driver will take you to the airport. Oh, I almost forgot. Luc asked me to give you this,' she added, handing Carrie a cheque. 'He understands that university can be expensive, and he wished me to tell you that he didn't want you to think he was unappreciative of your—'

Her face hot with chagrin and fury, Carrie broke in sharply.

'You can tell Luc that he can keep his money and that I don't want it—or him! Why should I? All he is—is a...a...an outdated character from a cheap operetta. A pantomime character who thinks he's something special because he gets to dress up in a uniform and call himself Prince! The only reason he still has this stupid bit of land is because no one else wants it. He's a joke! And you can tell him that I said so,' Carrie finished recklessly.

'How dare you speak so?' The Countess had lost her haughty, cool detachment, and was now furiously angry. 'My godson can trace his line right back over five hundred years, to the first Prince of S'Antander, who was granted this land as a gift from the Pope. His family have held it as a sacred trust against all adversity ever since. It was because Luc's grandfather allowed the Allied Troops to land here on our beaches that he himself was shot and lost his life! S'Antander is no mere puppet kingdom, as its ruling family have proved over and over again, and with your own ignorant words you prove—if it needed to be proved—how unworthy you are of sharing Luc's life.'

Much as she disliked the Countess, Carrie felt a tiny burn of shame. It was true that Luc's family did have a history and a tradition of supporting those causes they considered to be just and of benefit to humankind, but she was in no mood to acknowledge any good in Luc right now. In fact at this moment in time she felt that she hated Luc even more than she did his manipulative godmother! Ignoring the cheque the Countess was still holding out to her, she spun round on her heel and headed for the door, before her emotions could totally get the better of her.

CHAPTER ONE

'I WON'T say "be happy", because I know that you will be. I am so pleased for you both!'

Carrie hugged her beaming newly married brother and his ecstatic bride.

'Carrie, there is something Maria wants you to do for her,' Harry begged her urgently.

Enquiringly Carrie looked at the pretty dark-haired girl wrapped in her brother's arms.

'Please, Carrie, will you go to S'Antander and tell them that Harry and I are man and wife?'

'You want them to know?' Carrie questioned a little warily.

She had been taken completely by surprise by her beloved younger brother's announcement only a matter of days ago that he and Maria were to marry. After all, hadn't it always been a given that Maria was going to marry Luc?

While no official announcement of an engagement or forthcoming wedding had actually been publicly made, Maria herself had admitted that everyone expected her and Luc to marry—including Luc himself! But when Carrie had reminded Maria of this, Maria's response had been that her grandmother might have decided that she and Luc were going to marry, but Maria had absolutely no intention of being coerced into a cynical marriage of convenience—especially not now, when she and Harry had fallen so deeply in love!

'Of course I want them to know. I have nothing to

hide!' Maria answered, tossing her head proudly. She looked up at Harry, her whole face alive with her love for him as she added sweetly, 'Nothing and no one can part us or hurt us in any way now!'

Looking into their delighted faces, Carrie acknowledged that she envied them their confidence. And their shared love. It was plain that they were totally besotted with one another. Harry looked as proud as any ancient knight who'd rescued his lady from death by dragon. Though Harry was a man now, Carrie remembered, and not the boy she had cherished and protected as they grew up without a mother. The last thing she wanted to do was go to S'Antander, but Harry was looking at her pleadingly, and—as always—she couldn't bear to let him down.

'It's all right!' she heard Maria telling her confidently. 'I know that you and Luc don't get on, but you need not be afraid of seeing him. Luc…His Highness…will not be there! He's away in Brussels on important business. When he gets back he will be expecting me to be there, and I feel I owe him.'

Infuriated by Maria's assumption that she might feel fear at the thought of confronting Luc, Carrie told her fiercely, 'Maria, you don't owe that sexist brute of a puppet prince anything! Nothing at all! If he had had his way—'

Maria stopped her, her eyes filling with tears.

'He must be informed, Carrie. I know you don't like him, but Luc has never done me any harm. And…and it isn't just that!' Her chin tilting proudly, she went on, 'I want everyone at home to know how much I love Harry and how proud I am to be his wife—especially my grandmother.'

As she looked across at Harry Carrie's heart melted,

and she was reminded again of the almost maternal sense of responsibility as well as the great deal of sisterly love she felt for her younger brother. She was inclined to be a little bit too indulgent towards him, or so her friends claimed, but Carrie could not help feeling very protective of him, and she was delighted to see him looking so happy. His love for Maria and their marriage had given him a maturity that he'd perhaps previously lacked.

It was true that she had had her concerns about him recently, specifically where his work was concerned, and indeed, if she was honest... But she was not going to dwell on past problems now, nor take him to task for not confiding in her about his relationship with Maria. She was far too happy for him to do that!

Happy for him, but Maria's mentioning of her grand-mother had awoken some far from happy memories for herself!

Oh, yes, Maria's grandmother! Carrie's eyes suddenly glinted with a certain steeliness.

'Carrie, please,' Maria pleaded, 'There is no one else I can ask to do this for me. No one else I could trust...who understands just how things are at home in S'Antander...just how things are with Luc! If you would just go there for me and tell my grandmother. So that she can tell Luc.'

The very mention of Maria's grandmother was enough to raise the most ignoble and tempting thoughts in Carrie's mind!

She wasn't a naïve eighteen-year-old any more, she re-minded herself sternly. She was now a mature, confident and successful woman! A highly acclaimed economist, working freelance as a financial journalist.

Determinedly she tried to refuse, but Maria remained stubbornly insistent that Luc, His Serene Highness, ruler

of the small but perfectly formed principality of
S'Antander, had to be told that his prospective bride had
instead chosen to marry the man who had been her child-
hood playmate—Carrie's younger brother.

'Please, Carrie,' Harry begged her, and Carrie could
feel her resistance weakening.

A little ruefully she admitted that there was a part of
her that could not help feeling a certain degree of vale-
dictory triumph in being the one to carry the news to the
Countess that her granddaughter was not after all going
to meekly accept her grandmother's plans for her and fulfil her ambitions to make her Luc's wife.

After the misery of a cold, wet British spring, the warmth
that met Carrie as she stepped out of the airport at Nice
and set off to collect her hire car was indeed a welcome
relief.

Despite her fair English skin and straight silky shoul-
der-length naturally blonde hair, Carrie had never enjoyed
the discomfort of her home country's grey winter climate.
Perhaps it was the fault of all those school holidays spent
in S'Antander with her father—they had given her a taste
for the warmth of its sunshine!

Her father was retired now, and lived in Australia with
his second wife who, like him, had been widowed when
they met.

Carrie liked her stepmother who, having no children of
her own, had expressed herself delighted to be gaining
two adult stepchildren. Carrie's own mother had been
killed in a car accident when Carrie had been seven and
Harry only two. It had been one of the reasons why her
father had accepted the post in S'Antander, which had
included the benefit of proper domestic care for his young
children—although that had not stopped Carrie from

adopting her almost motherly attitude towards her younger brother.

Although Nice was its closest airport, S'Antander, which occupied a small strip of land between France and Italy, had been influenced by the Italian way of life as much as the French. Its people spoke Italian with a smattering of French names and vocabulary, and privately Carrie had always thought that there was a certain macho, Italian latinness about Luc himself.

The principality boasted a small seaport and harbour town, and its walled capital city was the site of an imposing castle which was both Luc's principal home—he also had a hunting lodge high up in the Alps, which he used as a winter skiing retreat—and seat of the country's government offices. It was set back from the coast, commanding a strategic position which overlooked both the main roads that gave access to the country.

Since the only way to get there was either to drive or to hire a private helicopter, Carrie had elected to drive. She might earn a very good living for herself, but it was not good enough to run to such extravagances as private helicopters! Unlike the new breed of entrepreneurs who were flocking to S'Antander to take advantage of its tax laws—just one of the innovative schemes and incentives that Luc was putting in place to attract income to the small principality!

'You're going *where*?' her agent and close friend Fliss Barnes had demanded in excitement when Carrie had told her what she was doing. 'You've got to do an article on the place whilst you're there, Carrie,' she had insisted. 'I've heard that it's awash with rich sports personalities and the like, and that you can't so much as buy a one-bedroomed apartment there for under a million!'

The young Frenchman who had handed the hire car

over to Carrie watched appreciatively as she walked over to it to check it over, admiring the length of her slender legs encased in a pair of low-slung jeans. A soft white tee shirt discreetly covered rather than hugged the rounded swell of her breasts, and the sunglasses she had put on to shade the cool jade-green of her eyes, whilst designer-logoed, were subtly discreet rather than flaunting their origins.

Quickly checking the time on the businesslike watch strapped to her narrow wrist, she unlocked the car. It was just ten a.m. That gave her time to drive to S'Antander and back again to the hotel she had booked herself in to for a brief self-indulgent stay before returning home.

Spring on the Côte d'Azur was a wonderful season, Carrie reflected, as she headed towards Menton, leaving the A8 behind to take the coast road.

After all, she was in no hurry to get to S'Antander—and revenge, so they said, was a dish best eaten cold!

She had never forgotten the cruelty of the way the Countess had spoken to her, and she had never forgiven the man who had given that woman authority to do so!

The naïve eighteen-year-old so desperately in love with Luc that he had filled her emotions and her thoughts to the exclusion of everything and everyone else had had to grow up very quickly since then.

A brief sadness darkened her eyes before she pushed her unwanted memories away as the once familiar countryside claimed her attention. Three years at university, followed by her father's retirement and remarriage, had ensured that there had been no need for her to return to S'Antander since the Countess had delivered Luc's dismissal to her.

A discreet signpost indicted the road to S'Antander's

border. Unlike Monaco, S'Antander had never touted it-self as a tourist attraction. Olive groves flanked the road, and in the distance she spied the turquoise brilliance of the sea. Winding down her window as she approached the border post, Carrie breathed in the warm fragrant air of the South, with its intoxicating blend of perfume and sun-shine.

A guard stepped forward as she stopped her car, dressed not in the pageantry of the country's historic military uni-form but instead in a much more serviceable police uni-form. Handing him her passport, Carrie waited as he in-spected it, and her, before handing it back to her.

It was only as she put the car in gear that she realised that she had been holding her breath.

Why? After all, Luc wasn't even in the country—never mind likely to have placed her name on a 'not to be ad-mitted' list! That was if he could even remember it!

As she drove further into the country Carrie was again entranced by its beautiful scenery. Centuries ago, before the country had been gifted to Luc's forebears, it had been owned by a reclusive order of monks. The monastery high up in the Alps was now an exclusive skiing centre owned by Luc, but the monks' careful husbandry of the land had been passed on to the people of the area, and as Carrie drove towards the capital she couldn't help but admire the neat, orderly rows of vines and the small olive groves.

It had been her own father who had encouraged Luc to make his people as self-supporting as possible. Every acre of agricultural land was used as productively as it could be, and Carrie could see the sun glinting on the plastic coverings that housed the country's much sought-after or-ganic fruit and vegetable crops

The road had started to climb now. Below her was the sea and the small port, whilst up ahead of her...

Her heart did a slow somersault as she spied the rich terracotta walls of the city towering over the landscape. Built on a rocky outcrop and surrounded by a fertile plain, the castle commanded an excellent defensive position. Carrie remembered how shocked her twelve-year-old self had been when Luc had shown her the castle's dungeons.

The steep incline of the road momentarily cut off the warmth of the sunlight, making her shiver in the coldness of the castle's imposing shadow. Even if she had not known the history of this place it would still have been easy to imagine how daunting it would have appeared to any invading force.

Grimly Carrie drove under the narrow, tunnel-like entrance into the city, blinking as she emerged into the brilliant sunlight.

Maria had told her that her grandmother would be in residence at her grace and favour apartment in the castle, rather than staying in her country villa, and so Carrie parked her car in the small town square and got out, squaring her shoulders before making her way through the market stalls towards the castle.

High up above the city, in the eyrie he had made his private office, Luc D'Urbino, His Serene Highness, Prince of S'Antander, frowned. He had just returned from Brussels, where he had been involved in protracted and complex negotiations with regard to his country's tax-free status, to discover that the political unrest which had been simmering between the traditionalist old guard of his grandfather's generation and their younger, far more politically radical opponents had reached boiling point.

Still frowning, he listened as his elderly cousin and Prime Minister told him tersely, 'The people want to see you married, Luc. The fact that you don't as yet have a son, an heir, makes them feel insecure! And besides, your wedding would help to take people's minds off all this fuss that's going on with these foolish young hotheads who are claiming that we are guilty of allowing criminals and murderers to make use of our country to hide their blood money, as they insist on calling it.'

Luc suppressed a sigh as he listened. From a personal point of view he completely sympathised with the opinions expressed by the so-called 'foolish young hotheads', but his position meant that he could not publicly take sides—and besides, he naturally felt honour-bound to protect not just his late grandfather's reputation but also the now sadly out of date and, because of that, vulnerable remaining members of the government who had been his grandfather's peers.

'I have already made it clear that as ruler of this state there is no way I intend to allow anyone guilty of profiting from the death of other human beings, or indeed any other illegal activities, to take advantage of our tax laws here,' Luc began quietly, and then stopped as he looked down from his window into the market square below.

There was a woman standing there with her back to him, the sun shimmering on the tousled silky fall of her blonde hair. Lifting a hand, she raked her fingers through it, as though impatient with its waywardness. Immediately he stiffened, his stance unconsciously that of a hunter, silent but awesomely effective, as if he instinctively scented a prey. There was something about her bearing, about the fiercely eloquent independence of it, that he instantly recognised.

'I am sorry, Giovanni, but I will have to discuss this with you later.'

Whilst his cousin watched in confusion, Luc thrust open the door and strode swiftly through it.

* * *

Carrie had no need to ask for directions to the Countess's quarters. She knew exactly where the suite of rooms she occupied was, just as she knew how to evade having to go through the formality of entering the main doors to the castle and making herself known to the impressively uniformed major-domo stranding guard there, behind the equally impressive-looking pair of traditionally uniformed, helmeted and musket-carrying sentries.

They were there more for show than anything else, their muskets unloaded, but that did not mean that either the palace or its occupants were not very efficiently and discreetly protected by the ex-military un-uniformed men who formed the bulk of Luc's security guards.

As she slipped through the small side door a hundred memories flooded back over her: the smell of the palace— a mixture of precious old furniture, works of art and ancient stone—and even more the smell of Luc, both before he had made love to her and after—a heady, dangerous mixture of male testosterone and those other indefinable scents that were his alone…

Or was she just allowing her imagination and her dangerous memories to play even more dangerous tricks on her?

Angrily Carrie closed her eyes, trying to blot out her unexpectedly sharply focused memories. Better that she remembered the icy hauteur of the Countess's voice, the contempt and the cruelty with which she had been treated—at Luc's behest after all—as well as the pain she herself had felt when…

'So it *is* you! I thought so!'

'Luc!'

Shocked, Carrie stepped back against the protection of the wall, her eyes widening betrayingly.

What was he doing here? Maria had insisted that he would be in Brussels.

And *she* had insisted that she was not afraid of seeing him, Carrie reminded herself! And she wasn't! No way.

'Well—an unexpected visitor indeed!'

Unlike her, Luc was dressed formally in a crisp white shirt and an expensive beige linen suit. His dark hair was immaculately groomed, his skin the same warm honey colour she had remembered during those long, aching nights when she had been so obsessed with the misery of losing him that all she had been able to remember was him.

His skin might look and feel warm, but his heart was icy cold—at least where she was concerned! Did the small whorls of body hair covering his chest still curl into small licks of curls, delicious to kiss in the damp heat of his bed? Did he still emerge from the shower looking like a Greek god, with the kind of physical proportions that…?

Aghast, and furious with herself, Carrie brought her thoughts to order. After all, she wasn't some wide-eyed innocent teenager now, awash with excitable hormones!

Lifting her chin, she told him briskly, 'Actually, I've come to see the Countess.'

Immediately Luc frowned.

'My godmother? She isn't here. She's away visiting her niece in Florence. What did you want to see her about? As I recall there was little love lost between the two of you,' Luc pointed out sardonically.

That he had known that and still allowed his godmother to humiliate her as she had done was all the reminder Carrie needed to make her bristle with antagonism and tell him challengingly, 'I've got a message for her. From Maria!'

She was supposed to be savouring this, Carrie reminded

herself, and her stomach suddenly dropped like a high-speed lift when she saw the way Luc was looking at her, his eyes narrowed intently, so dark that they looked almost black instead of the dark grey she knew them to be.

She could feel the silence stretching dangerously between them, taut with unspoken hostility and aggression.

'What message? Give it to me!'

He was so arrogant! At eighteen she might have been so idiotically adoring that she had accepted it, but not now! She could feel the swift burn of her own immediate antagonism. Carrie took a deep breath, too infuriated to think of delaying the retribution she was about to deliver.

'With the greatest of pleasure,' she told him 'She wanted you to know that she has married Harry, my brother.' She smiled unkindly at him. 'She loves him, and he loves her, and—'

CHAPTER TWO

'LUC let go of me!' Carrie demanded breathlessly, her face going hot with fury. But the relentless grip of his fingers on her upper arm did not relax one iota, and nor did the speed at which he was almost dragging her down the richly polished corridor, its walls ornamented with suits of armour and dangerous-looking heavy swords.

Carrie had a brief glimpse of the d'Urbino family crest above the imposing double doors before Luc pushed them open and half-dragged, half-thrust her into the elegantly furnished salon that lay beyond them.

She was, Carrie recognised angrily, in the main entertaining salon that formed part of the suite of private rooms occupied by Luc. Very little had changed since the last time she had been in this room; the silks and damasks might perhaps have faded a little more, and her own eight-year absence might have given her a more mature appreciation of the exquisite beauty of the room's furnishings, but that was all. The heavy silver-framed photograph of Luc's parents still dominated the highly polished sofa table, with Luc himself standing between them, a child of two.

Carrie remembered how she had so foolishly and fondly believed that the fact that both of them had lost their mothers at a young age somehow forged a special bond between them.

But Luc hadn't merely lost his mother—he had lost both his parents in the appalling atrocity of a terrorist

21

bombing incident in South America whilst they had been there on a visit.

'Maria has married your brother!'

There was no mistaking the cold fury in Luc's voice.

'I am sorry if you are disappointed.' Carrie couldn't resist taunting him.

'Disappointed?' Fury flared in the steel-grey eyes and his mouth thinned in recognition of her mockery of him.

'Still, I am sure you will quite easily find someone else to take her place.' The cynicism she felt darkened her own eyes and twisted her mouth.

Maria herself had made no bones about the fact that Luc's desire to marry her had been purely practically motivated.

'Luc does not love me,' she had told Carrie. 'But he has always been kind to me, and until I met Harry again and fell in love with him I had not really minded that ours would be a political union. Now, though, there is no way I could bear the thought of being married to anyone other than my dearest, darling Harry! And I am afraid that if I went back to S'Antander and told my grandmother and Luc that I couldn't marry him they might…'

'Force you to do so?' Carrie had finished for her, having no qualms about saying the words she had seen Maria, out of loyalty, was reluctant to speak.

'Luc has to marry someone.' Maria had unexpectedly defended him. 'The people expect it,' she had told Carrie simply. 'And of course he wants to have an heir.'

'The world must be full of women who would be only too eager to marry all this, Luc,' Carrie continued now, gesturing to the palace and the view beyond its windows. 'Oh, and you, of course. After all, you are such a catch, aren't you? A real-life prince, with so much to offer—

your arrogance, your snobbishness, your lack of any real emotional depth.'

'That's enough.' Luc stopped her coldly. 'But you are right about one thing, Catherine. It will be easy for me to find someone to take Maria's place. Very easy. In fact…'

The smile he was giving her was not a kind one, Carrie recognised, and something in his expression suddenly made her shudder, made her regret her emotional outburst of pent-up bitterness.

'In fact,' he repeated softly, 'I have already done so!'

Already done so? Now Carrie was shocked. He had already had a second choice waiting in the background? How typical of him, she decided contemptuously. But before she could voice her contempt he was continuing smoothly.

'If Maria is not to marry me, then, Catherine, you must!'

Carrie stared at him, speechless with shock and disbelief.

'What are you saying?' she demanded when she could speak, her voice cracking. 'If this is your idea of a joke.'

'It is no joke, I can assure you.' Unlike hers, Luc's voice was crisp and coldly assured.

'My people are in almost hourly expectation of hearing me announce my marriage,' he added grimly when she was unable to control her expression. 'There has been a good deal of gossip and public speculation on the subject, and they will naturally feel cheated now if I disappoint them. They believe that it is time for me to take a wife.'

'They are expecting you to marry Maria,' Carrie reminded him numbly.

'Who I marry is not of any real interest to them,' Luc returned with breathtaking arrogance. 'What concerns them is that I do marry!'

'Maybe so. But you are not marrying me,' Carrie told him fiercely, thankful to discover that she was beginning to recover from her initial shock.

'Oh, but I am, Catherine. As I have just told you, my people are expecting an imminent announcement that I am to marry. As you know, this is a very traditional country, and its older generation have certain fixed beliefs and expectations. They already feel that their values are being threatened by the younger people of S'Antander who, like all youth, believe that the only way of making progress is to dismantle that which previous generations have set in place.

'I am currently engaged in some extremely delicate and protracted negotiations, involving not only the views of these opposing groups within S'Antander but also the views of our ''guest'' residents, whose financial input into the country is not merely a valuable asset but also a necessity without which it would be impossible for us to fund such things as the extremely high standard of health care and education our people receive. My marriage will reassure the older generation that customs that are important to them are being respected and at the same time send a clear message to everyone else of my own commitment to my country and its future.'

Carrie stared at him in contemptuous disgust.

''No wonder Maria preferred to marry my brother. He might not have your wealth, or your position, but at least Harry is human, with human feelings and reactions. Not cold and calculating, like you.'

'I think you've said enough. In fact, I think you've said more than enough.'

Carrie could almost feel the steely implacability of his will-power reaching out to surround her, but stubbornly she refused to give in to it—or to him.

'I'm not an awestruck teenager any more, Luc,' she warned him. 'If you want a wife, then find someone else. You can't make me marry you!'

'No?' The look in his eyes sliced straight into her heart. 'I have recently heard some interesting things about your oh, so wonderful brother, Harry. Tell me? Are you still as protective of him, as devoted to him? Still as ready to fly to his defence? Of course you are.' He answered his own question tauntingly. 'Otherwise you wouldn't be here, would you?'

Without allowing her to answer he continued, 'He works for a merchant bank, I believe? Would it surprise you to know that he's been taking some very dangerous risks with the bank's clients' money? That he's been on the verge of making some very bad decisions? No, of course it wouldn't, would it?' he mocked softly. 'Not a devoted, caring sister like you! You were the first person he turned to when he realised the mess he was getting himself into, weren't you?'

Carrie felt as though her vocal cords had completely seized up. Unable to respond, or refute his savage indictment, she could only listen to him in growing shock and discomfort whilst an icy fist of fear embraced her insides. No one, but no one—apart from herself—could possibly know about the problems Harry had been having, the danger he had been in. But somehow Luc knew! Did that mean that he also knew...?

'How fortunate for him that he has such a devoted and clever sister there, not only able but also willing to help him out of a mess of his own making. A sister, moreover, who was prepared to risk her own career and professional reputation to do so. Because that is exactly what you did, isn't it, Catherine.'

'I don't know what you mean.' At last she had got her

voice back, but Luc was quite plainly unimpressed and unconvinced by her immediate denial.

'Liar!' he told her. 'You know exactly what I mean. Harry got himself into a mess and you got him out of it by advising him on what shares to buy to undo the damage he had done.'

Carrie looked away from him. How on earth had he managed to find out about that? She had sworn Harry to total secrecy, too shocked and worried for him when he had shamefacedly told her what had happened to be able to refuse to help, even though...

'He's my brother,' she responded woodenly. 'Naturally I wanted to help him.'

She hated the look of cynical satisfaction she could see in Luc's eyes.

'Even if in giving him that help you were guilty of insider trading?' he challenged softly.

Carrie heard her own audible indrawn breath of anguished despair.

'No, that's not true,' she protested 'It wasn't like that. It wasn't insider trading at all. I—'

'Not in your eyes, maybe, and perhaps not under the strict terms of the law. But, as I am sure you will agree, Catherine, in the right hands and with the right kind of publicity—or rather in the wrong hands and with the wrong kind of publicity—what you did could be made to look very bad indeed for you. For starters you'd probably lose your job and your professional status, and without you to rely on your little brother would certainly lose his. I could quite easily destroy you both, Catherine.'

'You'd do that? But what about Maria? Or is it Maria you really want to hurt?' she demanded.

'Certainly not! My proposed marriage to Maria was a diplomatic arrangement, not a love-match. She is the last person I would want to hurt in any way. As a matter of fact I am extremely fond of her, more than enough to keep a watchful eye on your young brother. If he does any-thing—anything—to hurt her or make her regret her de-cision to marry him—'

'You say that, and yet you're the one who is threatening to…to lose him his job,' Carrie reminded him fiercely.

'And you are the one who has the means to make sure that I do not,' Luc reminded her smoothly. 'The decision is yours, Catherine.'

Carrie stared at him. The room was warm, but she felt as though she were encased in ice. She could feel the coldness seeping into her bones, dripping through her veins, as deliberate and insidious as Luc's threat to com-promise and ultimately ruin her brother!

'You would do that?'

All the horror and disgust she felt was in her voice, but Luc seemed impervious to it.

'I am glad to see that you do not question that I can do it, Catherine. That shows an admirable grasp of reality. What would be even more admirable would be for you to show an equal grasp of the inevitability of our closer re-lationship. Don't worry. No one expects a modern mar-riage to last for very long. I am sure I shall very quickly realise the error of my ways in marrying you and we shall be free to go our separate ways.'

'You're threatening me with blackmail!' Carrie accused him, adding darkly, 'There's a law against that kind of thing.'

'You seem to forget,' Luc returned in an ominously silky tone. 'In S'Antander, I *am* the law!'

'You're despicable!' Carrie told him, her voice thick with loathing.

'The choice is yours,' Luc told her calmly. 'Either you agree to marry me or your brother—'

'You know I can't do that to Harry. I have no choice,' Carrie told him bitterly. 'You haven't changed, have you, Luc? I can't imagine why I was ever naïve enough to—'

Carrie stopped, her face beginning to burn.

'Go on...' Luc taunted. 'To...what, exactly? Beg me to take you to bed...to show you what it meant to be a woman...to...?'

'Stop it. *Stop it!*' Frantically Carrie covered her ears with her hands as she tried to blot out not just his cruel words but also the haunting and disturbingly clear images they were conjuring up inside her head.

'It's a bit too late to take on the role of injured innocent now, Catherine. After all, you never made any secret of the fact that you put what you learned in my bed to good use during your time at university.'

Carrie's teeth sank into her bottom lip as she forced back her instinctive response.

After all, it was true that she had written to her father describing her social life at university in terms which had made it seem as though her life was one long party—and that she was dating a different boy virtually every week. But nothing could have been further from the truth. The pain of Luc's rejection had caused her to retreat into herself and hold the opposite sex at a distance, concentrating instead on her studies. It had only been her pride that had made her write to her father pretending that she was having the time of her life! She knew that her father had never been entirely happy about her youthful passion for Luc.

'You're only eighteen, Carrie, with your whole life and its opportunities ahead of you,' he had told her. 'Whilst Luc already knows what his future and its responsibilities will entail.'

Her father, Carrie remembered, had felt that the task that lay ahead of Luc was an extremely daunting one.

'His grandfather ruled S'Antander as though it was still a medieval state,' he had once told Carrie. 'And it will be Luc's task to broker a way of bringing S'Antander into the twenty-first century. I certainly don't envy him!'

He had admired him, though; Carrie knew that…

'Luc, you're back! How did it go in Brussels?'

Carrie tensed as the salon door was suddenly thrown open, her breath catching in her throat as she stared in shock at the man who had walked in. His physical resemblance to Luc was so extraordinarily marked that it was obvious that they had to share the same blood—indeed, could have been brothers, if not twins!

Carrie didn't recognise him, though, and she frowned slightly, detecting an American accent.

'Oh!' As he saw Carrie he stopped speaking and looked enquiringly at Luc. 'I'm sorry, I didn't realise that you weren't alone!'

'It's all right, Jay. In fact you can be the first to hear our news and to congratulate me. Allow me to introduce you to my bride-to-be—Catherine Broadbent.'

His eyes were a different colour from Luc's, Carrie recognised as he focused on her. A bright warm blue instead of that cold steely grey, and she guessed that he was probably a couple of years younger in age—maybe a thousand years younger in terms of personality and self-will.

'Your bride-to-be? But I thought that Maria…' Jay stopped, looking uncomfortable.

'A common misconception,' Luc told him calmly. 'But, as it happens, Catherine and I go back a long way. Circumstances beyond our control led to us parting, but happily we have now rediscovered one another.'

'Well, I guess the old brigade don't mind too much who you marry, just so long as you do! They were beginning to get real twitchy that you might decide to step down and turn the country over to self-rule because of all the hassle you've been getting. I suppose as an American citizen I ought to claim that is what you *should* do, but I confess that I kinda like being able to boast that I'm related to a real-life ruling prince—even if it is on the wrong side of the blanket. I guess that tracing my family tree has to be one of the most rewarding things I have ever done.'

'You're a billionaire, Jay, and you've earned that success by your own efforts. I should have thought that was something to be far more proud of than any merit bestowed by a mere act of birth.'

'Careful, Luc, otherwise I might begin to believe that you think I got the best out of our shared gene pool. Remember, I know for a fact that you could have done exactly what I've done. You've got one of the best financial brains going, and don't forget I had the advantage of being handed my first million by my old man. All you inherited was a load of problems and a set of state regalia!'

Carrie's eyes rounded as she listened to the two of them subtly teasing one another. This was quite definitely a side to Luc she had never seen before.

'By the way, do I get to be the first to kiss the bride-to-be?'

Carrie smiled as he came towards her, but to her bemusement, just as he reached her, Luc put his hand on her arm and drew her to his side, keeping his own body between them.

'Catherine, allow me to introduce you to my second cousin—Jay Fitz Kleinburg. As you will probably have gathered, Jay and I have only recently discovered our shared relationship.'

'Yup, that's true. Luc's granddaddy was also mine! Only thing was he kinda neglected to put his name on my father's birth certificate! It's my grandmother I've got to thank for the ''Fitz'' in my name. Seems she'd read that in olden days in England royal bastards were given the prefix ''Fitz'' to their names, so she decided to do the same for my dad, and he passed it on to me!

'She only told us what had happened when she knew she was dying. Up until then she pretended that she'd married during the war and lost her husband! But I'm boring the pants off you. I guess what you both really want right now is to be on your own…'

Being on her own with Luc was the very last thing she wanted, Carrie acknowledged, but before she could say anything Jay was turning to Luc.

'I guess we can talk later about Brussels. You ought to know, though, Luc, that there's one hell of a lot of speculation going on amongst the tax exiles. Seems like most of them fear that you might be forced to make a change of policy, and give in to those young hotheads who are causing you so much trouble.'

'There's no question of that.' Luc's voice was terse. 'For one thing this country is almost wholly dependent on the income it derives from its tax exile inhabitants, although…' He started to frown. 'There are certain issues to do with the way things were conducted here during my grandfather's time which are going to have to be addressed.'

'Well, at least the news of your coming marriage will put a stop to the gossip going round that you intend to sell out to the money men wanting to take over the country and step down as ruler.'

As an economist herself Carrie was well versed in the financial status of S'Antander, but she had not realised that there was internal pressure on Luc regarding the way the country was run.

'Nice to meet you, Catherine.' Jay was smiling. 'You'll both have to come down to the yacht and have dinner with me—although I guess you'll both be pretty busy with formal engagements from now until the wedding. When is it to be, by the way?'

'At the end of the month. We shall be getting married on the same day as we celebrate our country's National Day. As you know, it is five hundred years this year since my family were given the country by the Pope. It seems fitting to celebrate my marriage at the same time.'

'As a symbol of your intention to see that the family continues to rule for another five hundred years?' Jay suggested.

Carrie was too shocked to speak. When Luc had told her that she must marry him she had had no idea he intended that marriage to take place so speedily! Maria had implied that her marriage to Luc was something that was to take place at some unspecified date well into the future.

Luc's cousin was leaving. Shaking herself free of the disbelief immobilising her, Carrie waited until the door had closed behind him before pulling away from Luc and telling him fiercely, 'This has gone far enough. We can't do this, Luc. It's crazy. No one is going to believe this marriage is anything other than a pathetic sham! We don't have the slightest thing in common!'

'No? What about this?'

Before she could say a word, Luc's hands had clamped on her upper arms and she was being jerked towards him. His head bent over hers, his body language predatory and dangerous.

It had been eight years since she had last felt his mouth against hers, since she had last tasted the sweet savagery of his kiss, since she had last felt the shocking pleasure of the hardness of his body, all lean muscle and bone, against her own, and in those eight years she had, she had believed, taught herself to forget the pleasure her foolish, immature self had felt at his touch, and to remember instead the corrosive pain of her disillusionment and humiliation.

And yet…and yet…

Some instincts…some senses…some memories were perhaps so deeply etched on a person's consciousness that nothing could ever erase them.

Her lips softened and parted, her brain clouded by a dizzying swarm of disempowering pleasure. A feeling like an electric shock jolted through her, heightening every one of her senses.

Desire, pain, anger—she could feel them all, and could have wept tears of aching anguish for the girl she had been and the memories Luc was forcing on her. It wasn't fair that he should do this to her—but then, when had Luc ever been fair? When had he ever done anything that wasn't motivated entirely by self-interest? He had taken her to his bed because he had desired her and then he had rejected her, dismissed her from his life like a toy he had grown bored with.

'No!'

Frantically, Carrie tried to pull away, but Luc was too powerful for her. His mouth possessed her with an easy strength, his tongue reinforcing his control of the situation, snaking between her lips, thrusting powerfully into the tender, vulnerable warmth she was trying to withhold from him.

The fog clouding her brain became a white-out of

sheeting panic. She should not be feeling like this. She lifted her hands and pushed against Luc's chest, at the same time wrenching her mouth from beneath his. Abruptly he released her, freeing her to drag air into her aching lungs.

'Odd. You still kiss like an innocent.'

The way he was looking at her made Carrie's stomach lurch with anxiety. That steely grey gaze was far too sharp and penetrating.

Defensively she snapped back at him, 'Actually, I wasn't doing any kissing. But of course it's typical of you, Luc, that you were too intent on doing what you wanted to notice. You are the last man I would ever want to kiss. In fact, you are the last man I would ever want in any way at all.'

'Really?' His tone was even more sardonic than the look he was giving her. 'That's not what this says,' he told her mercilessly, and he reached out and very deliberately ran his finger down the curve of her breast, to where her nipple jutted tightly against the fabric of her tee shirt.

Carrie's face flamed in angry humiliation.

'That doesn't mean anything,' she told him fiercely, pushing his hand away. 'I—'

'You what?' Luc challenged her 'You react to every man who touches you in that way? Well, let me warn you, Carrie, that from now on, for as long as our marriage lasts, there will be no other men in either your life or your bed.'

'You can't tell me what to do—' Carrie began, but Luc stopped her immediately,

'You have no option other than to do as I say, Carrie,' he said gently, but there was no gentleness in his eyes, just a hard, implacable determination that warned her he meant every word he was saying. 'Because if you don't, both you and your brother...'

She couldn't allow him to carry out his threats against Harry, Carrie acknowledged, no matter how strong her feelings of outrage and disgust towards him were.

'Very well,' she told him through gritted teeth. 'As you say, it seems that I have no option, Luc. But I promise you that I shall hate every single day, every single minute, every single second I spend shackled to you, and I shall do my utmost to make sure that you hate them too.'

'My charming wife-to-be...so loving, so tender, so complaisant.' Luc taunted her. 'I am sure that ours shall be a match made in—'

'Hell,' Carrie supplied savagely for him.

'So much passion! But then, you always were...passionate.'

The look he was giving her was an open insult, but somehow Carrie managed to bite back the words she was longing to throw at him.

CHAPTER THREE

THE soft swish of her bedroom curtains being opened followed by a bright shaft of morning sunlight woke Carrie from the sleep she had only finally fallen into a couple of hours previously. For most of the night she'd been kept awake by a turbulent inner warfare in which her instinct for self-preservation had battled with her lifelong elder sister instinct to protect her younger brother—and lost! She had eventually fallen into an exhausted sleep, knowing that she could not expose Harry to Luc's diabolic cruelty!

Her mouth compressed now as she was dragged back into the dilemma which had tormented her all through the previous evening and into the soul-searching long night.

Nothing would have given her a greater sense of satisfaction or...or fierce justification than to expose Luc for what he was: to state publicly the contempt she held him in and to give him a taste of just how it felt to be helpless within someone else's power, devoid of pride and self-respect. But how could she, knowing the power he had to destroy her younger brother?

It was not the farce of marriage itself that bothered her; she knew Luc well enough to know that he meant exactly what he had implied by that throw-away comment about modern marriages being of short duration. Once Luc's purpose was served their marriage would be brought to a very swift and uncompromising end, and of course it would not be a marriage at all, merely a pretence to suit Luc's own ends.

36

No, it was the fact that he had the power to force her to do as he wished that she hated, the fact that once again she was allowing herself to be used and manipulated to suit him!

The maid had finished opening the curtains and was standing at a respectful distance from her bed.

'My name is Benita. I am to be your maid. If you wish to have breakfast here in your suite…'

Her English was perfect, if slightly stilted—it had been Luc who, during the years of his minority, had insisted that S'Antander's schools taught all its pupils English as a second language. Even then he had been strong-willed enough to oppose the old-fashioned views of the Regency of Ruling Elders, who had felt that such a course was an unnecessary expense.

'S'Antander is a very small country,' he had told them. 'It is only to be expected that many of my people will want to go and live and work in the wider world, and when they do it is only right that they should be equipped with the means to do so. They must have the opportunity of learning a second language!'

Carrie remembered sardonically now how much she had admired him for his stance when her father had related the episode to her! But at that time, of course, she had been only too inclined to admire anything and everything that Luc did. As well as admiring Luc himself. Admiring? She had adored him, worshipped him…'

'Thank you, Benita. Breakfast would be—' she began, and then stopped speaking as the door to her bedroom was thrust open and Luc strode in.

The maid, round-eyed and pink-cheeked, took one look at him, dipped a nervous little curtsy and fled, leaving

Carrie to glare unwelcomingly at him and to curse the
fact that she had not seen fit to pack something to sleep
in!

The beautifully soft towelling robe she had found in
her bathroom and left last night on the chair beside the
huge six foot square bed she was now occupying had
already been removed—no doubt by the attentive maid!

A little unexpectedly Luc was wearing a body-hugging
white tee shirt, a pair of easy fitting jogging bottoms and
running shoes.

She remembered that he had always been insistent on
adopting a healthy lifestyle. His own private suite of
rooms included its own indoor swimming pool, and he
was a virtually championship class skier and an Oxford
Blue.

Carrie well remembered the intoxication of crewing for
him on board his racing yacht, and recalled that he had
even played polo for a while, whilst at university in
England.

But though he might work to keep healthily fit, it was
Mother Nature who had originally given him his superbly
muscled and even more superbly male body, Carrie decided grimly. She was the one who was responsible for
the havoc that Luc created, the desire and wanton longing
he aroused so easily in Carrie's own sex.

Put Luc in any kind of clothes and any kind of setting,
no matter how humble, and he would immediately stand
out and catch women's eyes.

Of course she wasn't the least bit impressed by the air
of arrogant superiority that cloaked him—quite the opposite. Nor was she susceptible enough to have her heart
almost stop beating at the very thought of him wearing
the dress uniform that denoted his position as the
Commander of the country's small military force, never
mind actually seeing him doing so!

Her days of feeling her insides melt with a hot rush of desire brought on by the thought of seeing Luc dressed in a pair of shiny top boots, tight-fitting trousers, white trousers and a military-style jacket of rich blue with yards of heavy gold braid were long since over!

She could still remember, though, how Luc had teased her by offering to prove to her that the impressive jacket was worn next to bare skin.

However, there was nothing remotely teasing in his voice now as he told her sharply, 'Our betrothal is to be announced at noon today, in the castle square, along with the date of our wedding... Oh, and my cousin Jay has invited us to join him on his yacht this evening, for an informal celebration of our betrothal. The press will be informed that, in view of the rekindling of our passion for one another, we could not bear the thought of a lengthy engagement.'

'So you still intend to go ahead with this farce?' Carrie challenged him fiercely. 'I should have thought that a night of sensible reflection would have shown you—' she went on loftily, only to be stopped as Luc advanced towards the bed.

'You haven't changed, have you, Catherine? You still like playing dangerous games. When you were a teenager it was obvious what you hoped to achieve, but I do not understand just what it is you expect to gain by baiting me now. Unless, of course...'

As he waited Carrie felt her face begin to burn. It was true that when she was younger she had innocently attempted to provoke a masculine reaction of desire from him, but for him to throw that at her now—!

'You are despicable, Luc,' she threw at him, enraged. 'Totally and utterly despicable!'

Although he shrugged her comment aside, Carrie could see the glint in his eyes.

'You have, I trust, something suitable to wear? A formal business suit, perhaps, in view of your career? You know, Carrie, I must say how surprised I was to learn what an excellent degree you obtained, in view of the lifestyle you led at university. You obviously have your father's flair for economics, although I suspect from the tone of your articles that you are more in sympathy with the views of certain young hotheads amongst my own people than those of the establishment. But then you always were an intensely passionate creature.'

'No, Luc,' Carrie corrected him bitterly. 'What I was was a foolishly vulnerable young girl. But fortunately I had the good sense to realise how empty and…and valueless the relationship we had was.'

Carrie watched as his mouth thinned. It surprised her that he actually knew so much about her, but presumably her father had informed him of what she was doing.

'Be careful,' he warned her silkily, 'otherwise I might be tempted to show you that there could be certain aspects of a relationship between us that you—'

'No way! Never!' Carrie denied vehemently. 'I might once have been foolish enough to…but I was very quickly cured of that error of judgement, Luc.'

'In the arms and the beds of the other men you gave yourself to so eagerly when you left here for university?'

'How dare you presume to speak so sanctimoniously about my sexual history? Every summer the glossy magazines carry a new story about your latest piece of "arm candy", Luc—models, actresses, pop singers…'

'The people you are talking about are new tax exile residents to this country. It's not my fault if the popular press chooses to deliberately misconstrue matters, and besides, it is not—'

'My business?' Carrie finished for him. 'No, it isn't, and neither is my sexual past any business of yours!'

Not for anything would she have him know of her stubborn insistence on reading each word published in those magazines, describing the beauty of his female companion and his attentiveness towards her. But it had only been to reinforce to herself how much better off she was without him!

And as for his comments about her clothes! Well, yes, she did have a plain, businesslike designer suit in her case!

'Your sexual past might not be my business, but so far as your sexual present and future is concerned, Carrie, I warn you now—'

'*You* warn *me*! You might think you can act however you want in this…this soap operetta of a country of yours, Luc,' Carrie began furiously, pushing herself up in the bed in a sudden flurry of angry activity, 'but there is no way—'

Halfway through gesturing vigorously to underline her point, Carrie suddenly realised that the bedclothes were sliding off her body.

Automatically she made a quick, protective dive for them. But Luc beat her to it, his lean fingers tanned, nails immaculate but wholly masculine, curling round the edge of the covers and wresting them away from her, holding them flat to the bed.

His grey gaze on hers pinned her into immobility.

Carrie could feel the colour come and go in her face as it burned with furious emotions.

'So, the girl I remember slept in a nightshirt printed with puppy dogs and bows. Only a very sensual and sexually confident woman sleeps naked in a strange bed, Carrie.'

'Or one who just happens to have forgotten to pack her nightdress,' Carrie returned acidly.

She could feel the warmth of the sunshine on her bare breasts.

'You don't sunbathe topless.'

Now Carrie could feel her face really burning. How had he managed to notice that, when so far as she was aware he hadn't even glanced at her breasts? He had kept his gaze fixed on hers, as though her body was of so little interest to him than it didn't even merit a brief look!

'My last holiday was in America. They don't favour topless sunbathing at the resort where I stayed.'

'So your partner was able to enjoy the knowledge that only he was able to fully view your body?'

'My "partner", as it happened, was a woman-friend,' Carrie told him pithily, her eyes flashing storm signals at him. 'Not that it would have been any of your business if it had not been.'

So why had she felt such a furious need to leap to the defence of her virtue? Carrie wondered grimly. It didn't matter what Luc thought of her any more, did it? And besides, as she had just reminded him, he hardly lived like a monk, did he? At least not if the popular press were to be believed!

Angrily she tugged hard on the bedclothes, trying to drag them upwards to cover her naked breasts. When Luc refused to allow her to do so Carrie took refuge in the only protection left to her: the acid sharpness of her contempt.

'I suppose there's something of the voyeur in all men, a sort of base instinct, but I must say that I'm surprised to see it surfacing in you, Luc. After all, you've always made it quite your thing to elevate yourself to a higher and more rarefied plane than everyone else, haven't you? Your Serene Highness!'

Luc cast her a narrow-eyed look, and she was satisfied to discover that her words had made an impact as she read the flicker of grim male fury in his eyes. But retaliation was swift and merciless as he dropped his gaze to her breasts and studied them with an insolent thoroughness that made her face burn. 'You obviously wanted to flaunt yourself in front of me. I didn't want to—'

Carrie stopped him angrily. 'Flaunt myself? You've got to be joking.'

He frowned, suddenly and unexpectedly releasing the bedcovers to slide back his jacket cuff and glance at the elegant gold watch he was wearing.

'You have two hours in which to have breakfast and get yourself ready. I have some telephone calls to make.'

Carrie gaped at him, thrown by his abrupt change in demeanour, only realising as he started to turn away from her that she had not taken the opportunity to cover herself up.

Pink-cheeked, she quickly did so.

'We shall meet in the Green Salon at eleven-thirty,' Luc told her coolly. 'My press secretary is already preparing the announcement of our betrothal.'

Carrie gave a small sigh of satisfaction as she studied her reflection in the huge floor-to-ceiling mirrors in the dressing room of her suite.

Her classic tailored suit was perfect for such an occasion, if perhaps a little bit on the formal side.

A wide grin curled her lips and made her look like a naughty urchin.

And that was why the suit was still hanging in the

closet whilst she was wearing a pair of clean but very old and very faded narrow-fitting jeans topped with a tee shirt cropped just above her waist to display a couple of taut, creamy, warm inches of bare female skin.

A much heavier application of mascara than she would ever have normally worn, combined with a very pale pink lipstick and enough product in her hair to glue wallpaper, had transformed her from her normal sleek, soignée self into a very passable replica of the kind of hip-swinging, head-turning modern and feisty ladette currently so much in vogue on the celebrity circuit.

It was the kind of look she would never normally have adopted, and Luc was bound to loathe it, she decided gleefully.

Twenty-five past eleven. She had timed it perfectly!

Grinning to herself, she opened the door to her suite and stepped into the corridor.

The Green Salon was one of the less formal of the palace's state rooms, if such a description could be applied to a room decorated with enough gilt rococo and plasterwork to make one's jaw drop. The carpets had been made at the famous Aubusson factory, especially to match the design of the plasterwork ceiling, and the room had two sets of double French doors which opened out onto an elegant balcony which in turn overlooked the beautiful private gardens enclosed by the walls of the castle. On formal occasions liveried footmen were posted either side the elegant double doors, as with the other formal state rooms.

Carrie was relishing the impact her appearance was likely to have on Luc. Her behaviour might be childish, but it was the only way she had of demonstrating how she felt about what he was doing—the only way she had of rebelling against it and him without hurting her brother.

She had almost reached the bottom of the flight of stairs that swept down to the impressive oval hall when the double doors to the Green Salon were thrust open and Luc strode out, coming to an abrupt halt as he saw her.

For a moment neither of them moved. Carrie could see the fury in Luc's eyes, and a tiny quiver of triumph shot through her.

It was like watching a storm approach, she acknowledged, and a fine shiver galvanised her flesh. She had that same sense of smelling sulphur in the air, of feeling unmistakable threatening tension and brooding danger; feeling the tiny hairs lifting at the back of her neck.

'Is this some kind of a joke?'

The question was delivered in tone so flat that it immediately increased the tension by several notches.

'Excuse me?' Carrie feigned innocent ignorance, but the light of battle was fierily visible in her eyes.

'You know perfectly well what I mean,' Luc snapped icily. 'Your clothes—!'

'Are my clothes.' Carrie stopped him sharply. 'These are my clothes, Luc,' she repeated, 'and this is me. I don't intend to change either to suit you. You can take me or leave me, as you wish. It was your choice to blackmail me into this abhorrent betrothal and marriage, but how I dress is my choice! Oh, and I still prefer Carrie to Catherine, Luc. It may not be as formal, but it's a name I'm comfortable with.'

Carrie watched at his mouth compressed.

'I have seen the photograph accompanying your articles, *Carrie*, and I know perfectly well that this is not how you normally appear in public. Your hair…'

Carrie frowned. He had seen her work…read it? Something unwanted and dangerous was trying to flower into painful life inside her. Fiercely she smothered it.

'You don't like it?' She threw him a challenging look and tossed her head. 'It's the latest thing.'

'It looks as though you've emptied a pot of wallpaper paste on it,' Luc told her uncompromisingly, 'and you certainly can't appear in front of my people looking like that. They would be affronted…insulted…'

'Luc… What are you doing? Luc, let go of me,' Carrie demanded when he suddenly strode towards her and took hold of her arm, turning her round and almost marching her back up the stairs.

'If you don't stop it I shall pick you up and carry you bodily, Catherine,' he warned her, when she continued to struggle.

Carrie stiffened.

'You—'

You dare, she had been about to say, but the look he was giving her made her swallow the challenge unspoken.

By the time they had reached her suite Carrie was out of breath. Luc, she noted resentfully, was not.

Thrusting open the door, he pushed her inside and, gripping her arm, locked the door.

'You are pushing me to my limits, Carrie,' he told her, tight-lipped.

'So what? That's your problem, not mine. I don't—'

Carrie gave a small gasp as she was suddenly yanked almost off her feet and into his arms. His mouth covered hers, smothering her furious tirade, and he kissed her with an angry, almost savage ferocity that ignited her own banked-down anger.

This was a kiss like no other she had ever experienced, Carrie recognised distantly as they fought one another for control, mutual antipathy and resentment fuelling a white-hot passion that burned its imprint into her every bit as much as the feel of Luc's mouth against her own.

She could feel her heart racing, thudding as adrenalin poured through her whole body. She was not in flight mode, but quite definitely up for a fight. A feeling she told herself was righteous determination shot through her—a fierce, wild clamour of sensation and urgency that masqueraded dangerously as something perilously close to desire.

But of course she did not desire Luc, and he did not desire her either—even though she could feel the sudden shocking and familiar hardening of his body against her own. Somehow one of his hands had slid up under her top and was pressed flat against her spine, whilst the other cupped her breast, its thumb rubbing demandingly against her nipple.

His body might have hardened, but hers now moved closer to him, and the anger that had fuelled her fevered reaction to his punishing kiss began to transmute dangerously into a very different kind of passion.

Frantically Carrie pulled away from him.

'Have you any idea how much I loathe and despise you?' she demanded furiously.

'Oh, that's what you were trying to show me, was it?' Luc taunted, but Carrie could see that his own chest was rising and falling just that little bit faster than it should have been.

Not that it really gave her any satisfaction to know that he had been momentarily physically aroused. No, what she actually felt was a sense of disgust. Yes, that was it! Disgust…and shock that she herself could have been vulnerable enough to allow herself to react to him!

'You have half an hour,' she heard him telling her grimly. Either you go and do something about your appearance yourself or I shall do it for you. And don't make the mistake of thinking I don't mean it, Carrie. If I have to dress you myself then I shall, but I promise you that if I do you won't like it.'

Trying not to betray her apprehension, Carrie pulled away from him. She could tell that he wasn't joking.

In the bathroom, she stripped off her jeans and top and then quickly cleaned off her make-up. Wincing, she tugged a brush through her hair.

Her hands were trembling as she reapplied a discreet amount of eye shadow and mascara. Thankfully her hair had already settled back down to its normal style.

Feverishly she glanced at her watch…Ten minutes gone! It wouldn't take her more than another ten to slip into her suit, and then…

Her suit… Carrie froze as she realised that her suit was still in the wardrobe—outside the locked bathroom door—and that Luc was also waiting on the other side of the door! Nervously she chewed on her bottom lip until she realised how many minutes she was wasting.

Grabbing a towel, she wrapped it around her self and unlocked the door, putting her head round it.

Luc was leaning against the door to the suite, arms folded across his chest.

'Ready?' he demanded.

Carrie shook her head.

'I need my suit,' she told him.

'Where is it?

'In the wardrobe,' she replied, watching in bemusement as, instead of telling her to come and get it, he strode over to the wardrobe and opened it, removing the suit.

'This it?' he asked her.

Silently Carrie nodded her head, tensing as he brought it to her.

'Five minutes,' he warned her as she took it from him.

Suddenly, for no reason at all, her hands were trembling so much that she wasted valuable seconds trying to zip up her trousers. Why on earth was she feeling so quivery and nervous inside? Certainly not because Luc had kissed her!

'Time's up.'

Carrie gave a gasp as Luc yanked open the bathroom door and surveyed her in silence.

'It's either this or the jeans,' Carrie warned him as she stepped past.

'Just a minute…'

Warily Carrie watched him. An icy wash of sensation sent a sickening surge of emotion through her as he removed a leather jewellery box from his pocket.

'You're going to need this,' he told her coolly.

Carrie knew what the box would reveal. After all, she could still remember the first time Luc had shown her the traditional D'Urbino betrothal ring. Then she had gasped in wide-eyed disbelief as she had stared at the huge emerald surrounded by glittering diamonds, thinking she had never seen such a beautiful and awe-inspiring ring.

Then, though, she had been a teenage girl, imagining how it must feel to have a man like Luc slide such a ring onto one's finger, proclaiming to the world his love and commitment.

Now she saw the ring in a very different light. The coldness of the betrothal Luc was forcing on her matched the icy brilliance of the diamonds, just as the ring's heavy weight matched the weight of oppression she felt she was under.

'You're trembling…'

The cool, almost mocking words stung.

'Yes. With anger,' she retaliated. 'What you are doing is despicable, Luc.'

'No. What I am doing is what I have to do, for the benefit of my people,' Luc told her coldly. 'But then you always were too hotheaded, too…too emotional to recognise that sometimes one has to put one's duty above one's own desires.'

'It's twelve o'clock,' he announced, whilst Carrie was still frowning over his words.

Disturbingly the ring fitted her perfectly, but she felt acutely conscious of its presence when, five minutes later, Luc tucked her arm through his, holding her in a way that was both regal and proprietorial as he waited for the shrill fanfare of trumpets to die away on the warm air before guiding her out into the brilliance of the sunshine and the flash of the photographers' cameras that awaited them.

Carrie heard the formal announcement being made, and shivered despite the mild temperature. The gathering crowd were cheering and clapping. Or at least some of them were.

Towards the back of the group being contained by Luc's men, was a vociferous and angry band of young people, chanting slogans and waving banners declaring that they wanted the right to remove from the country blood money brought into it by foreigners.

In an effort to protect herself from the reality of what was happening Carrie tried to focus on what they were chanting rather than listen to the flowery speeches being made regarding her and Luc's supposed future marital happiness.

It took another fanfare of trumpets to bring her attention back to Luc, but she still wasn't prepared for it when he turned to her and lifted her left hand to his lips, his gaze on hers as he kissed her fingers and then slowly lowered his mouth to hers.

The crowd went wild, cheering and clapping, and the

photographers' cameras went into ecstatic overdrive—and Carrie felt as though she wanted to howl like a hurt child.

This should not be happening. It was a desecration of everything that such a moment should be. It was...

Luc had lifted his mouth from hers. He placed his hand beneath her elbow and told her quietly, 'It is expected that we should walk amongst the people so that they can share our happiness and congratulate us in person...'

Carrie ached to make a sarcastic retort, but she could already feel Luc's fingers digging warningly into her upper arm through the jacket of her suit.

'Highness, I really think it would be better for you to return inside the palace,' advised an elderly, stern-looking man whom Carrie recognised as being one of the group of men who had counselled and advised Luc during the years of his Regency. 'Your grandfather would never have tolerated such insurgency, and I really would advise that this young rabble who persist in their ridiculous claims are punished swiftly and firmly. I recommend a ban on any kind of demonstrating in public—perhaps even a curfew. You know my views.'

'And you, Geraldo, know mine,' Luc returned calmly, giving a small smile to lighten the sternness of his semi-rebuke. 'I appreciate your advice and your concern, of course, but the people have a right to express their feelings, and—'

'If they carry on like this everything your grandfather strived to establish for our country will be destroyed. Without the guaranteed secrecy of our banking laws...'

Luc still had his fingers curled restrainingly around Carrie's arm, and Carrie felt their grip tighten briefly in reaction to the older man's angry outburst. But when she turned her head to look at Luc his expression was calm and unreadable.

'I respect and revere everything that my grandfather did, Geraldo, of course. But times have changed and we need to change with them. Even our Swiss neighbours are under pressure from the EC to change their banking privacy laws. When I was in Luxembourg last month I was asked some particularly searching questions about the subject. We can discuss all this later, but for now my people wish to see my wife-to-be and to congratulate me on our coming marriage. I do not intend to disappoint them.'

For a moment Carrie thought the older man was going to renew his objections. She could see from the dull flush of colour staining his thin cheekbones that he wanted to do so, but obviously something in Luc's expression was preventing him.

'Very well! It is your right to make such a decision, after all. You are the ruler of S'Antander...'

'Indeed,' Luc agreed gently.

'But let me at least have those rabble-rousers removed...'

Carrie saw that Luc was shaking his head.

'Leave them be, Geraldo. They have a right to their views, after all, and to be allowed to express them.'

'Yes, but at one of your three-monthly courts, not at a public event like this.'

Luc merely smiled and shook his head, before turning to lead Carrie into the square.

Carrie admitted that Luc's apparent tolerance and leniency towards the demonstrators had surprised her. Was he really as open to listening to their complaints as he was implying, or was his 'tolerance' simply a tactical ploy?

As they walked past the guards Carrie tensed when they stiffly presented arms. It was all so overdone and unnecessary, she told herself grimly. They were drilled to perfection and dressed like toy town soldiers. But deep down inside a small part of her rebelliously recognised not just the pageantry of the display but all the centuries of history that lay behind it.

A gust of wild cheering blew towards them as they circled the sunshine-filled square, and to her consternation Carrie actually found silly, emotional tears stinging her eyes as people stretched out their hands to touch her: children, with happy, excited upturned faces, older women, small and sun-wrinkled, looking adoringly at Luc whilst their menfolk bowed their heads in silent respect.

'May God bless you,' Carrie heard women murmuring to her. 'And may he give you fine sons and beautiful daughters.'

'It is our Prince who will give her those,' Carrie heard one man chuckling to his wife, and ridiculously she could feel her face starting to burn.

At the far end of the square, in front of the demonstrators, a line of cavalrymen sat immobile astride their immaculately groomed horses.

They had covered two sides of the square now, and were closer to them.

As an economist Carrie was reasonably familiar with the situation regarding countries which operated as tax havens for the very wealthy, and she frowned when she read some of the messages on the demonstrators' placards. But before she could say anything there was a sudden outbreak of raucous booing from them as they approached.

'I thought you said that your people wanted to see you married.' She could not resist taunting Luc as the demonstrators made their feelings plain.

Carrie could see that a scuffle had broken out amongst

the crowd as some of the more traditional onlookers started to object to the insults the demonstrators were directing at Luc. Some rotten fruit was thrown, falling short of its target and splattering onto the immaculate stone flags. One of the cavalry horses jiggled at its bit and started to prance restively. A small group of the demonstrators pushed their way to the front of the crowd, right behind the horses, and started to jeer noisily at Luc and Carrie.

Regally, Luc ignored them.

Carrie noticed that one of the demonstrators was carrying a small child and had put him down the better to throw something into the square. Out of the corner of her eye she saw the small boy squeeze under the cordon— and then, horrifyingly, one of the hurled missiles hit one of the horses, causing it immediately to panic and rear up at the very same time as the little boy toddled beneath its raised hooves.

Carrie automatically sucked in her breath and lifted her hand to her mouth. Like those in the crowd who could see what was happening and shared her fear she gave a shocked gasp.

Abruptly Luc released her, running swiftly towards the child and sweeping him up into his arms and safety just as the horse's hooves came crashing down.

The crowd let out an exhalation of relief and a woman started to cry in a noisy outburst of pent-up anxiety. The child's father, white-faced now, and suddenly shrunken, stood pressed up against the cordon as Luc walked over to him, holding the little boy.

Carrie could feel the crowd's silence as it watched the unspoken contact between the two men. No one who had witnessed what had happened was in any doubt that Luc had saved the child's life, and at potentially no small risk to his own.

Against her will Carrie felt a huge lump in the back of her throat. With that one gesture of rescuing the youngster and handing him over to his father Luc had demonstrated all that was best about the paternality of his role as ruler, showing himself to be just and caring and strong enough to protect those weaker than himself. This served to humble and silence his detractors.

Someone in the crowd gave a cheer, breaking the solemn stillness, and it was quickly taken up by everyone else so that within seconds the whole square was ringing with the people's approval and admiration.

CHAPTER FOUR

CARRIE frowned as she looked round her bedroom. The bed, the chair, the chaise, and even the floor itself were covered in expensive-looking carrier bags, boxes and dress bags, whilst Benita, the young maid who had attended her earlier in the day, was standing amongst them looking both excited and bemused.

'What on earth is happening?' Carrie demanded. 'What is all this stuff? Where has it come from? What is going on?'

'It is His Serene Highness's orders,' Benita explained breathlessly. 'He requested that a new wardrobe was to be sent up from Cannes for you.'

'Oh, he did, did he?' Carrie responded, an angry gleam in her eyes.

'There will be much excitement amongst all the design houses.' The maid was sighing happily. 'They will be ecstatic to have a new princess to dress...'

And even more ecstatic at the thought of how much 'dressing' her was going to cost, Carrie thought grimly.

As she moved closer to the bed she could see the designer names discreetly inscribed on some of the bags.

How dared Luc behave so high-handedly—so arrogantly? If she wanted new clothes she was perfectly capable of deciding so herself, and choosing and paying for them!

Grimly she started to gather up some of the bags and carry them over to the door.

'These are to go back to Cannes immediately,' she told

the maid crisply. At any other time the look of disappointment on the girl's face would have amused her, but right now she was far too angry for amusement!

'But, please, you cannot mean that. The Prince has commanded this himself.'

Carrie's mouth compressed.

'His Highness may command his people, and he may even command the shopkeepers in Cannes, but he does not now and never will command me. All this…everything is to go back—and right now!' she announced forthrightly.

The maid's face crumpled in bewilderment.

'But tonight there is to be a grand evening on the yacht of Mr Jay Fitz Kleinburg and you have nothing to wear! All the other ladies will be in very beautiful clothes, and you will not. But you are to be the wife of His Serene Highness and it is not fitting that they should look more elegant than you.'

There was outrage as well as confusion in her voice.

'My cousin, she is a maid at the villa owned by Gina Pallow, the American actress, and she tells me that Ms Pallow is to wear a brand-new gown created especially for her. Yes, and the other ladies will be in very fine gowns as well. Mr Jay Fitz Kleinburg—he always has many beautiful ladies on his yacht. Many, many celebrities of great beauty have now come to live in S'Antander.'

'I have a linen dress with me. I shall wear that,' Carrie announced unrepentantly.

With a theatrical flourish the maid stalked over to the dressing room and returned with Carrie's dress.

'If you mean this…' she began disdainfully.

'Indeed I do,' Carrie confirmed. 'And—'

She broke off as her bedroom door was suddenly thrust

open and a tall, forbidding-looking elderly woman came in, flanked by a pair of nervous, hovering attendants.

The Dowager Countess—Maria's grandmother! Refusing to be cowed by the severe look she was receiving, Carrie lifted her chin and met the Countess's haughty gaze with an equally cool one of her own.

With the merest flick of an eyebrow the Countess skewered Carrie's maid into frozen apprehension.

'Leave,' she commanded her coldly, then ignored her as she turned to wave her own attendants out of the room along with Carrie's maid.

'So—it is true!' the Countess began without preamble. 'You have had the effrontery to come back to S'Antander and, even worse, you have somehow persuaded Luc to agree to this farce of a betrothal. It is just as well that I decided to return from Florence earlier than I had planned. Luc is to marry Maria—'

'Unfortunately I am afraid that he cannot—unless she proposes to commit bigamy,' Carrie told her sweetly 'You see, Maria is now married to my brother.'

Oh, the pleasure of seeing the Countess's expression! Her face held shock, disbelief and fury—all of them vied for supremacy, but none of them could come anywhere near competing with the bitterness and the obvious loathing the Countess clearly felt for her, Carrie acknowledged.

'You're lying…'

Carrie gave a dismissive shrug.

'If that is what you wish to believe, then of course you are free to do so. You know, I am not surprised that Maria felt unable to tell you of her plans herself. And I do believe that she feels for the first time in her life she is properly loved. All she's ever been to you is a pawn, isn't it? You have never loved her for herself, as my brother does, only for what you can use her for. Well, I am sorry, but it is too late. Maria is married to my brother and I am here.'

'You do not need to tell me what *you* are doing here,' the Countess claimed contemptuously. 'You have come to inveigle your way into Luc's bed for a second time. Well, it will not work. I cannot understand how you have managed to persuade him to announce his betrothal to you, but I promise you I mean to find out—and once I have done so...'

Carrie said nothing. Let the Countess find out for herself that, far from inveigling Luc into a betrothal, he was the one who had forced the betrothal on her!

'I would not put it past you to have deliberately persuaded my poor granddaughter to become involved with your wretched brother just so that you could steal the place that rightfully belongs to her. You are not fit to hold so high a position. You do not begin to have the faintest idea of how to conduct yourself as the wife of a man of Luc's station in life. Just look at you—the way you are dressed. Never would I have permitted Maria to wear such clothes—jeans...'

Carrie's temper was almost at breaking point, but it was her pride that stung the most from the Countess's contemptuous words. So the Countess did not think that she was fit to marry Luc, and she didn't think that Carrie knew how to conduct herself for such a role, how to dress herself for the position... Well, she would soon show her just how wrong she was about that, Carrie decided furiously.

'And what are all these?' the Countess demanded, glaring at the confusion of bags and boxes.

'My new clothes,' Carrie informed her with relish. 'Luc has bought them for me.'

The Countess's face tightened in anger. 'I see! You

have obviously not lost any time in persuading Luc to spend money on you! How long have you been in S'Antander? One day…two…?'

Carrie had had enough.

'It was Luc's idea, not mine,' she told her flatly. 'And anyway, as you have just pointed out yourself, since I am to be his wife it is only fitting that I should be dressed accordingly.'

A sudden surge of rebellion filled Carrie, causing her to add in a theatrically dramatic tone, 'Naturally I don't want to let Luc down, and as his wife…'

Carrie could see how much her words were infuriating the other woman, even whilst a part of her was shocked at her own aptitude for pretence.

This unfamiliar aptitude for acting had obviously taken her over, Carrie decided, and to further infuriate the Countess she found herself pouting and tossing her head as she looked over to the bed, giving a loving, lingering look at the collection of boxes and bags she had previously rejected.

'I just hope that Luc has remembered that I don't have any proper jewellery. After all, when we attend this dinner tonight, on Jay's yacht, it is important that my appearance befits my new role. I must say I can't wait for us to be married. Our wedding is to take place at the end of the month—when the country celebrates its fifth centenary. I have heard that the crown jewels of S'Antander are exceptionally magnificent…'

The Countess's face had turned an unpleasant mottled shade of purple.

'You will never marry Luc,' she told Carrie furiously. 'Never.'

Carrie winced as she heard the door slam behind her. She had truly burned her boats now, she recognised shakily. There would be a heavy price to pay for the fury and pride which had driven her to react to the Countess in the way she had, and to make matters worse there was certainly no way she could appear at tonight's party in her plain black linen dress now!

Luc had got his way again.

Carrie sat back on her heels whilst her maid, overcoming the formality she had exhibited when she had first attended Carrie, lovingly hung up the last of the clothes she had unpacked.

There was nothing quite like mutual female admiration for beautiful clothes to bond two women together, Carrie acknowledged wryly. As they had sorted through the bags together, Benita had quickly responded to Carrie's questions to her, revealing that she had just finished university and that she had taken this job at the palace for the summer to fund her gap year abroad before settling down to her chosen career in law.

And what clothes! Reluctantly Carrie had to acknowledge that they were truly beautiful—and carefully chosen. She now had a wardrobe to cover virtually every occasion, from the most exquisite formal gowns right down to two pairs of sexy skinny jeans and an equally stunning denim skirt. Carrie had not been able to resist smiling to herself as she had unwrapped those items. So much for the Countess's snooty claim that Luc's wife could not wear jeans! But then, of course, there were jeans and jeans— and there was no way that Luc would have chosen these clothes himself!

'Do you think that perhaps for tonight this gown?' Benita suggested, very quickly warming to her new role.

Carrie looked at the gown she was holding in front of

her. Heavily beaded and cut daringly low, it was magnificent, but…

'No. I think that for tonight this one will be better,'
Carrie told her, going over to the wardrobe and removing
a simple cream silk-satin column dress with a high draped
neckline and an elegantly fluted skirt.

'It is very plain, and not at all sexy,' Benita objected.
And then blushed…

'I—I am sorry,' she semi-stammered. 'I am being too…
I should not…'

'No… I prefer you to be honest with me,' Carrie told
her firmly. 'And you are right—this gown is not sexy, but
it is the one I want to wear.'

Carrie checked her watch. It was time for her to go down-
stairs to the Green Salon and meet Luc prior to their departure for Jay's yacht. He had sent her a message earlier,
announcing that he had some work to do and would not
therefore be able to join her for dinner, but he had invited
some of his closer advisers and their wives to have drinks
with them prior to the party so that they could be introduced to Carrie.

The huge ring on her left hand still felt heavy and
strange. Benita had vehemently denied having provided
anyone with information as to what size of jewellery or
clothes Carrie wore, but someone had made a very ac-
curate guess.

The dress she was wearing fitted her perfectly, skimming her body to fall in a soft pool of expensive fabric
that flared out into a soft fishtail behind her. And, thinking
of behind, there was certainly something very skilful, not
to say a little bit magical, about the way the tiny row of
gathers at the back of the dress just below her waist

caused it to fit and flare in an unexpectedly seductive way around her, Carrie acknowledged.

She had decided to wear her hair up, in a simple and soft style that complemented the gown and also gave her an opportunity to show off the pretty diamond stud earrings her father had give her for her twenty-first birthday.

Just in case the spring evening turned out to be cool, she was taking the wrap which had come with the gown with her.

It was seven-thirty. Time for her to go down to the Salon.

Carrie could feel the small hush that fell on the room as the two footmen threw open its doors for her to enter.

There were probably about forty people gathered in the room, a mere handful for its size, but Carrie saw only two of them.

One was Luc, who stood facing her. He was wearing a dinner suit, and to her chagrin Carrie felt her heart twist and turn, almost as though a knife had pierced it with pain.

The other was the Countess, who was dressed in a heavy satin very formal gown whilst her hands and throat shimmered with diamonds. But not even their icy glare could match the look in her eyes as she stared at her, Carrie acknowledged.

Ridiculously, she had a sudden compulsion to run to Luc, and indeed discovered that she had actually taken several steps towards him before she could stop herself.

As she hesitated he stepped forward himself, extending his hand to her. The sudden movement of the Countess's hand momentarily drew her attention, and she recoiled as she saw the hatred and contempt in the older woman's eyes. Carrie's chin lifted, and determinedly she walked towards Luc, keeping her gaze on him until she had reached him.

'Carrie.'

The warm softness she could hear in his voice was not for her benefit, Carrie reminded herself as he drew her hand through his arm and turned her round to the waiting courtiers

Ten minutes later Carrie told herself that she must be becoming blasé, since she no longer felt the need to stifle nervous giggles when someone bowed or curtsyed to them—or rather, to Luc.

The people she was being introduced to were the old guard of the Court, she recognised. Men who had been friends of Luc's father and in some cases his grandfather. These were stiff, stately, old-fashioned gentlemen who wore their medals and their years with pride, accompanied by wives who reminded Carrie dauntingly of her boarding school headmistress.

There were one or two slightly younger faces amongst their ranks, but Carrie could see how the older group hung together, holding themselves aloof from the younger.

'And, of course, my godmother, the Dowager Countess, needs no introduction to you, Carrie,' Luc was saying.

'No, indeed not,' Carrie agreed grimly.

Ignoring Carrie completely, the older woman turned to Luc and began, 'Luc, I cannot—'

Before the Countess could continue, Carrie put her hand on Luc's arm and leaned towards him, saying softly, 'Luc, darling. You've been so busy introducing me to people that I haven't had time to thank you for my wonderful gift.'

Doe-eyed, Carrie leaned closer to him, aware of both the Countess's fury and Luc's own look of dark-eyed watchfulness.

'You really are too generous,' Carrie continued huskily. 'This beautiful gown and all my other lovely clothes.' She could feel Luc's arm stiffening as she gripped it with her hand and reached up to him, cupping her other hand along the slightly rough edge of his jaw as she pressed a pseudo-loving kiss against his skin.

Out of the corner of her eye she could see the slightly shocked faces of the courtiers, but their shock was nothing, she suspected, to Luc's. His whole body froze. Normally she would never have behaved in such a way, but it was worth it just to see the manner in which the Countess's rigidly corseted bosom swelled with fury.

'I shall have to thank you properly...later,' Carrie breathed, throwing in a look of misty-eyed adoration just for the pleasure it gave her to see both Luc's hard look of query and the Countess's inability to contain her bitterness.

'What was all that about?' Luc demanded ten minutes later, when they were alone.

'What was what about?' Carrie asked innocently.

It was very satisfying to see the way his mouth compressed.

'Don't play games with me, Carrie. You know what I mean.'

Carrie gave a dismissive shrug.

'I just wanted to thank you for the clothes...' Carrie continued coyly.

'Luc, I know this isn't the time, but if I could have a word about today's demonstration...'

It was one of the younger courtiers, his look apologetic as he interrupted them.

'I have heard that this rebel group intend to bring a question to your next open Court, and that they will demand to know whether or not we have allowed people who are in breach of Human Rights laws to hold funds in S'Antander. It is an issue that is bound to attract a good deal of international interest, on both sides.'

Carrie listened in attentively. She was familiar with the country's tradition of its ruler holding three-monthly open Court sessions during which any of his subjects could raise any matter they wished with him, but it was her interest as an economist that was focused on what was being said.

Any changes made to S'Antander's financial rules would have serious repercussions for its economy, but she also knew that—quite rightly, in her opinion—there was a growing swell of concern and objection amongst right-thinking people about the way in which some of those who had deposited funds in secret in S'Antander and other countries' secret bank accounts in the past had acquired that wealth.

'There are two separate issues here, Carlo,' Luc was saying. 'On the one hand we have our new influx of modern tax exiles, who simply want to avoid paying excess taxes in their own countries and have therefore made their homes here, and on the other we have those who do not live here but who have deposited their wealth in the secret bank accounts that were allowed and encouraged to be opened during my grandfather's time.

'Certain authorities are pressing very hard to have that old system declared obsolete and made illegal, as you know, and there is all too likely to be a huge and international legal battle on both sides of the argument.'

'Luc, we must find a way to get these people to remove their accounts.'

'So you say, Carlo, but there are others here who take exactly the opposite view and say that legally we cannot do such a thing and indeed that we *should* not, since the revenue our country earns from managing such affairs is very considerable.'

Carrie frowned as she listened. Luc had not said which side of the argument he supported, she noticed grimly. Personally she was all for having such people outlawed and their ill-gotten gains returned to their rightful owners, but she knew that her views would most likely be viewed by Luc as a little on the reactive and emotional side.

Even so, half an hour later, when they were on their own, seated together and being chauffeured to the harbour and Jay's yacht, with the partition between them and the chauffeur closed, Carrie couldn't resist challenging Luc by saying, 'I notice that you didn't agree with what Carlo had to say.'

'Whereas you, of course, did?' Luc returned urbanely, throwing the challenge right back at her.

'Yes, as a matter of fact I do,' Carrie agreed hotly. 'I think it's totally unacceptable that anyone should profit from other people's suffering...'

She meant what she said, of course, but Carrie knew that she was also making a dig at Luc personally.

For a moment she thought he wasn't going to deign to reply, but then he said coolly,

'Has it occurred to you, I wonder, that the money this country has earned by providing secret bank accounts for people helped to pay your father's wages, and therefore indirectly funded your own education?'

Carrie could see the gleam in his eyes as she turned her head to stare at him.

'Nothing to say?' Luc asked her.

Carrie turned her head to look out of the window of the car. His comment had shocked her, but logically she was unable to refute the truth of it.

'Situations change,' Luc told her. 'When my grandfather became ruler this country was a very poor one; my grandfather wanted to improve the situation. He took advice on how he could best maximise the country's assets and he looked to other smaller countries to see how they had benefited from their tax and financial laws. For him the issues were much more simple than they are now. He was the ruler of a country that was facing extreme poverty. He was responsible for people who had little education and even less hope of improving their situation, and so he did what he could to help them.'

Luc's voice became stern. 'His first thought was for these people—his people. His view was in many ways very parochial. Nowadays I know we take a more global view, but I cannot and will not decry what my grandfather did. It is thanks to him that S'Antander's people now enjoy the high standard of living they do, thanks to him that their children receive a world-class education, thanks to him that we enjoy excellent health care...'

'You were the one who put in place the health and education improvements,' Carrie couldn't help pointing out.

'Maybe so, but the fact that I was able to do so financially is thanks to my grandfather. I will not have him turned into an ogre. Nor will I allow everything he did for this country to be ignored or reviled.'

He sounded so grimly stern that Carrie felt herself give a small shiver. This was a side to Luc she had always sensed existed, even as a girl. He had always spoken very passionately about his commitment to his country, but back then she had romanticised that passion. Now she was aware of a grim and unshakable coldness, a purposefulness about him, a steely self-control which he imposed upon himself as well as on others.

For Luc, S'Antander would and must always come

first—even before his own needs and desires. Duty and responsibility would govern him, rather than love, and to her surprise she discovered that the knowledge actually made her feel slightly sorry for him. Maturity had a great deal to answer for, she acknowledged wryly, if it could make her feel sympathetic to Luc.

Her sympathy was short-lived though, when he suddenly demanded, 'Anyway, Carrie, what was that less than edifying little sideshow at the reception all about?'

'What do you mean?' Carrie demanded, but of course she knew, and was glad of the darkness of the limousine's interior to conceal her burning face.

'I mean the unnecessary and slightly nauseating display of "gratitude" you staged. The Catherine I remember would never have behaved in such a way—but then, of course, I appreciate that that girl no longer exists. Probably never did exist.'

Carrie shot him a murderous look.

How dared he criticise her? If she was not the same, then whose fault was that? Who was the one responsible for 'changing' her, through his cruel and hurtful treatment of her?

'Of course it may be that the type of man you normally consort with thoroughly enjoys being the recipient of such sickeningly false attention, but…'

The men she normally consorted with! Oh, how Carrie longed to put him right on that issue. But a deeply ingrained instinct for self-preservation cautioned her against doing so. Instead she seized on another avenue for defence and retribution.

'You're right about one thing,' she acknowledged recklessly. 'There's no way I would normally allow you—or any other man, for that matter—to patronise me by insinuating that I am not capable either financially or in any other way of selecting my own wardrobe—but then the men I normally ''consort'' with, as you put it, would never dream of behaving in such an insulting or unwanted way. Given free choice, there is nothing I would have liked more than to dump the whole lot at your feet and tell you where to put it, but I have my brother to think about—as you never seem to tire of reminding me.'

She was fibbing. There was no way she was going to admit to Luc that her pride had been rattled by his over-bearing godmother!

'So, that promise to thank me more personally in private...'

'You're quite safe, Luc.' Carrie stopped him sharply. 'You find the thought of my kisses offensive and un-wanted, and believe me that's nothing to what I feel about yours. Sexually, you are the last man I could ever want.'

The car had pulled to a halt, the chauffeur had switched on the interior lights and was getting out to open the rear doors.

Carrie knew that her face was still burning with cha-grin—but at least she had made her feelings clear!

CHAPTER FIVE

S'ANTANDER'S steep-sided harbour could easily have modelled for the perfect Mediterranean port. Its surrounding hillsides were dotted with elegant villas, the port town itself still very much as it had always been, since no modern building developments had been permitted. In the daylight the quaint houses could be seen as painted in a variety of toning Tuscan colours, but at night the small town looked just as delightful, almost as theatrically perfect as a Hollywood stage set, Carrie decided as she tried not to be impressed by the elegance of the obviously carefully renovated area, with its collection of small bars and eateries all facing onto the square fronting the marina itself.

The water was full of expensive-looking yachts, but none of them came anywhere near matching the size of the one they had pulled up next to, Carrie admitted as the chauffeur held open the door of the limousine for her.

What she was looking at was goodness knew how many million pounds' worth of floating perfection, Carrie guessed, and she hesitated a little uncertainly in front of the gangway.

Luc had caught up with her, and as she felt his hand cup her elbow she pulled fiercely away from him.

'Stop that,' he commanded her immediately. 'This is a public occasion, Carrie, during which we shall be watched.'

'Luc, until two days ago everyone was expecting you to marry Maria. They are hardly going to imagine that you and I have fallen madly in love with one another.

You're His Serene Highness, ruler of S'Antander, and of course they will assume that you are marrying for reasons of necessity rather than reasons of desire.'

'It is not unheard of, you know, for necessity and desire to go hand in hand on occasions. You are to be my wife, Carrie, and I expect you to behave accordingly.'

'Really? Well, I have to tell you that your expectations are not of very much interest to me, Luc, and of even less importance.'

Carrie gave a gasp as his fingers suddenly bit into the flesh of her upper arm. He was bending down towards her, and her stomach gave a fierce kick of reciprocal antagonism, mixed with something dark and dangerous and unnamable as she saw the anger glint in his eyes. But before he could say anything to her Jay had appeared at the top of the gangway, calling out warmly to them.

'Great—you've made it! Welcome on board.'

As he took her arm Jay kissed Carrie on the cheek, causing her to turn and look at him and to reflect again how amazingly alike he and Luc were physically.

'Come on, let's go down to the main salon and I can introduce you to everyone. They're all dying to meet you, Carrie. Especially the ladies. They've all heard the news about your betrothal, and of course about Luc's rescue of the child. That was very heroic, Luc, and should go a long way to smoothing down the problems you've been having with your rabble-rousers.'

Carrie could already hear the hum of conversation and laughter coming from the enormous elegant salon they were approaching, and she was irritated with herself when she suddenly felt a small frisson of nervousness. What, after all, did she have to feel nervous about?

Rather a lot, she recognised wryly as she and Luc walked in through the salon's double doors and a swift silence fell on the room, its occupants' attention wholly focused on them.

'Ladies and gentlemen, may I present my guests of honour? My cousin Luc, His Serene Highness, Prince of S'Antander, and his beautiful bride-to-be, Miss Catherine Broadbent.'

Whilst they were waiting for the applause to die down Jay summoned one of the circulating waiters and handed Carrie a glass of champagne. The waiter offered Luc one.

Nervously Carrie took a gulp and felt the bubbles burst against her tongue. The champagne was blissfully dry—and she guessed horrendously expensive. The décor of the salon would not have disgraced a mansion and she blinked a little, wondering if the paintings she could see on its walls were the original works of art she suspected them to be and not merely excellent copies.

Having the comfort of being financially secure was a goal most people naturally and understandably aspired to, Carrie acknowledged, but to be in possession of this kind of wealth....

Luc was also extremely wealthy, of course, but not in quite the same way as his American cousin, she suspected shrewdly. Luc's wealth was part and parcel of his heritage, something that Luc would consider to be a sacred trust, whereas Jay's...

No wonder Luc had referred to him as a billionaire!

'Luc, darling...I do hope that you aren't expecting me to curtsy to you! After all, we know one another far too intimately for that, don't we?'

Automatically Carrie focused on the woman who was smiling at Luc, immediately recognising her as one of Hollywood's hottest new talents.

Carrie was slim, but this woman was minute, her waist the smallest hand's breadth and her legs, which were clearly discernible beneath the fine silk of her long dress, so incredibly slender that to Carrie they looked as fragile as those of a young colt.

Only her breasts showed any sign of womanliness, being so unexpectedly voluptuous that Carrie suspected they had been surgically enhanced. Like her pout, which was so full and ripe that Carrie found she could not take her eyes off the gleaming pinky scarlet lips. And if she could not do so, then what effect must they have on a man? Luc certainly seemed to find both them and their owner fascinatingly compelling, Carrie acknowledged.

The actress had managed to position herself at an angle to Luc that not only allowed her to place one beautifully manicured hand on his arm but also to virtually turn her back on Carrie.

Had she in reality been Luc's fiancée, Carrie suspected that right now she would be feeling a little insecure and very annoyed.

'Luc, you are very naughty, you know,' teased the starlet. 'You promised me that you would take me to Monte Carlo, to the casino, and you have still not been to see my new villa. You will love it, Luc. I instructed the designer to incorporate all your ideas—especially that one about having a private terrace with its own Jacuzzi. I can't wait to show it to you! I have told my director that S'Antander will make the most perfect setting for my new film, although no mere actor could ever come anywhere near comparing with you, Luc. You are so much the real thing...'

She gave a husky soft laugh and rubbed her fingertips intimately against Luc's arm before lifting herself up on tiptoe and kissing the side of his jaw.

'Oh, dear—look. Now you are covered in my lipstick,'

she murmured, lifting her finger to rub it away and somehow managing to brush it against his mouth.

Unable to drag her eyes away, Carrie wondered if Luc would give in to the deliberate incitement to take her finger into his mouth. If he did…

Carrie's eyes widened as Luc's fingers curled round the actress's wrist, holding it as he stepped a pace back from her.

'Carrie, allow me to present to you Ms Gina Pallow.'

Carrie could see the hostility in the other woman's eyes as she glared at her.

'Oh, Luc, I feel so sorry for you,' she cooed. 'Everyone has been saying how much they would hate to be in your position, and feel forced into a diplomatic marriage.'

She gave him the full benefit of her crimsoned mouth in a theatrical pout before deliberately throwing Carrie a dismissive look.

'I should have thought that since you are the ruler of S'Antander you could do what you like. After all, I already know how much you enjoy doing what you like, Luc…when you like…'

There was no mistaking the deliberately provocative declaration the other woman was making! Carrie knew that Gina was putting on this show for her benefit, and was suddenly furiously angry that Luc should allow her to be humiliated in such a fashion.

Burying her nose in her glass of champagne, Carrie took a deep gulp, and then another. This actress obviously intended to make a no holds barred claim on Luc. Well, Gina was welcome to him! Carrie decided. However, she was not going to stand insipidly by and be insulted—as she fully intended to make *very* clear!

Still ignoring Carrie, Gina was asking Luc huskily, 'Do

you like this new perfume I'm wearing, Luc? It's been especially blended for me.'

Personally Carrie was finding the heavy musky scent extremely overpowering. Instinctively she wanted to wrinkle her nose and put some space between them, but Luc seemed to have no complaint at all about the actress moving even closer to him!

Carrie's arm was still formally linked through Luc's, and irritably she started to tug it away.

'Please excuse me.' Carrie gave them both an openly false smile. 'But I really do need some fresh air.'

She released herself from Luc's grip and walked calmly towards the exit, only allowing herself to give in to the fury trembling through her once she was safely outside the double doors.

How dared Luc parade his...his mistress in front of her like that and expect her to stand meekly at his side ignoring what was going on? He might be a prince, theirs might be going to be a marriage made out of necessity and not love, but she was damned if she would allow herself to be humiliated in public like that. How many of the other guests on the yacht had either guessed or suspected that Luc and the actress were lovers? And how many, if they hadn't been before, had now been alerted to what was going on by Gina's very public display of possessive sensuality towards Luc?

Sexually, Carrie didn't care one jot how many liaisons and lovers Luc had had, but she had her pride, and to stand there whilst Gina flaunted their relationship in front of her, whilst she flirted with him and fondled him...and whilst Luc said and did nothing to deter her...

She was, Carrie discovered, actually grinding her teeth!

'Carrie?' A little warily Carrie watched as Jay approached her.

'I was just going to go up on deck to get some fresh air,' she explained.

'Good idea. I think I'll come with you.'

He said it so warmly that Carrie couldn't object.

'I see that Luc's been landed with Gina. She's a bit of a man-eater, I'm afraid...'

As he spoke Jay was leading her up to the open deck.

'Oh, I don't think Luc is objecting very hard,' Carrie responded lightly.

As they reached the deck Carrie could see the brief speculative look that Jay was giving her.

'Ouch...a rose with thorns! You are going to be so good for Luc.' He grinned, adding when Carrie looked surprised, 'Luc's a great guy, and I think the world of him, but his life means that sometimes he lives in a bit of a rarefied atmosphere. He needs someone strong enough to ground him and inject a healthy dose of reality into things for him! Something tells me that you are just the woman to do that. Don't get me wrong. I like Maria. She's a great kid—a sweet girl, in fact. But too sweet for Luc. He needs a woman, not a girl—a woman with a bit of salt about her. A woman strong enough to treat him as a man and her equal, a woman to understand and support him, to be there for him!

'I must say I don't envy him his responsibilities,' Jay continued more seriously. 'He's stuck right in the middle of one hell of a tricky situation, and it's going to take one hell of a lot of nerve and guts to get safely through it. On the one hand he's got a bunch of hotheads yelling "off with his head", so to speak, and for self-rule if he doesn't give them what they want, and on the other he's got a whole bunch of stiff-necked, stubborn old diehards who refuse to acknowledge that times have changed. I just hope that between them they don't force on Luc a Judgement of Solomon.'

Carrie frowned enquiringly.

'What I mean is…' Jay explained. 'Well—you know how when the two women both claimed the same baby Solomon said that the child should be cut in half and divided equally between them the real mother was prepared to abandon her child rather than see it harmed?'

Carrie nodded her head.

'I would hate to see Luc abdicate because he felt it was in S'Antander's interests for him to do so. Anyone can see that it most certainly isn't! He is a very gifted and caring leader, and in my opinion this country would be in a hopeless mess without him. I guess the best thing he can do right now is to give both sides something else to think about—and that, of course, is where you come in,' Jay told her, giving her a disarming smile. 'A royal wedding followed by a royal birth ought to do the trick!' he chuckled.

A sudden spurt of wind caught at Carrie's wrap, tugging it free of her body. Immediately Jay reached out to grab it, tucking it protectively back round her.

Automatically Carrie turned towards him to thank him, and then froze as she saw Luc standing several feet away, watching them.

There was no mistaking the look he was giving her, Carrie recognised, and Jay too turned, looked at him, and immediately excused himself, telling Luc cheerfully, 'I'd better get back to the salon…'

'I see that you haven't changed,' Luc told her, tight-lipped, as soon as they were alone. 'You and I are to be married, Carrie, and if you think—'

Carrie stopped him with a sharp burst of bitter laughter.

'Oh, that's rich,' she told him fiercely. 'You allow your

lover to practically eat you alive in front of me, never mind the fact that she couldn't wait to let me know that you and she are intimate, and then—'

'That's just Gina. She doesn't mean any harm.'

'Are you blind, Luc? Of course she means harm. She—'

'Be careful Carrie,' he taunted her. 'Otherwise I might think that you're jealous, that the sight of Gina touching me and the thought of me touching her, kissing her...'

'No! Never!'

Carrie's chest rose in fierce agitation as she battled with her fury. In the half-light she could see Luc's head turn, but it was several seconds before she realised that what had caught his attention was her body, that he was looking speculatively at her breasts and the tight crowns of her nipples, clearly visible against the smooth fabric of her gown.

That anger could be so dangerously erotic was a piece of self-discovery she could very well have done without, Carrie acknowledged grimly as heat flooded her body in a drowning, drenching surge of physical arousal that left her shocked and shaken, confused and savagely in denial of what she was feeling.

'I've already shared your bed, Luc,' she reminded him wildly, 'and what I experienced there taught me that you don't have anything to offer I could ever be jealous about. If you were to...to touch me or...or kiss me now it wouldn't mean a thing to me. In fact, I'd probably be physically sick,' she told him furiously.

'Is that a fact? Well, let's just see, shall we?' Luc's voice was tight and low, savage with bruised male pride.

Carrie turned to escape, but it was too late. Luc had goaded her and she had goaded him in return. She ought to have remembered that Luc hated being the loser in anything or in any way!

Luc had somehow managed to enclose her so that she had her back to the rail of the yacht. His hands gripped it on either side of her.

They were standing body to body, and she could feel the slow, heavy, measured thud of his heart as well as the quick, frantic, panicky race of her own.

A furious torrent of jaggedly painful emotions which she was in no way ready to deal with poured through her, totally confounding and infuriating her. That sharp, aching, intense sensation that was so shamingly familiar! Did she really not remember just what it was? Of course she did! But that had been then and this was now, and just because she was feeling it now that didn't mean what it had meant then! She didn't want him. How could she? That white-hot surge of feeling…of need of…of reaction had been nothing more than a momentary lapse—a trick played on her senses by the pressure she was under, she tried to comfort herself.

But all the time her body was reacting to him. And the mix of physical desire with emotional hostility and fear, and the toxic brew that resulted, made her head throb with pressure.

His head bent towards her and she could see the movement of his eyelashes, thick and ridiculously long for a man, as he lifted lazy lids to look silently at her.

'Do you remember the first time I kissed you?'

The unexpectedness of the abrupt question shocked her, but she couldn't reply to it. Instead her body shook violently.

'You were just eighteen,' Luc continued, 'and you'd been looking at me…at my mouth…with big hungry eyes for weeks, saying without words just how much you wanted the feel of it against yours. Everywhere I went, everywhere I looked I saw you—watching me with those yearning, pleading eyes, begging me…'

Carrie could feel her fingers curling into hurt, angry fists. He was stripping her pride bare, revealing her youthful vulnerability with the skill and clinical expertise of a surgeon wielding a scalpel, peeling back layers of protective flesh to expose the soft, tender, fragile thing that had been her most secret essence. Her heart, her love, her self.

Carrie could feel the raw ache of pain burning her throat. She wanted to cry so badly her chest felt tight with the intensity of it, but there was no way she was going to do so.

Instead she willed herself to dredge up her defences and lift her chin as she shrugged and told him, 'So I had a crush on you?' She tried desperately to sound nonchalant.

'That was a crush? You *begged* me to take you to bed. You told me—'

Carrie knew she could not endure much more.

'I was eighteen, Luc.' She stopped him forcefully. 'More of a child than a woman. I thought you were Mr Perfect—the sun, moon and stars and then some all rolled into one. For heaven's sake, I practically had an orgasm every time you looked at me,' she told him flippantly, praying that her directness would slice through the very dangerous effect he was having on her.

But to her dismay, instead of reacting to her remark with cool disdain, as she had hoped, he looked at her for a very long time—so long, in fact, that she was struggling to endure that look.

'I know you did!' he said softly. 'I used to look at you and see that little telltale quiver beginning in your body. Your eyes would give it away first—darkening, the pupils dilated—and then your throat would tense and you'd be struggling to swallow. Next your breasts would swell, and your nipples harden so much that their reaction to me would make you blush. But by that time it would be too late for you to control what was happening to you, and you'd give a little shiver, and I'd look at you, and…'

Carrie couldn't stand any more, and even though she knew she was playing into his hands by doing it she still could not prevent herself from trying frantically to push past him.

It was the wrong thing to do! She knew that immediately, even before he took hold of her with a look in his eyes that told her how triumphant he was that she had given him the excuse to do so.

Love might transmute lust into something finer and more life enhancing, but anger had the opposite effect, Carrie acknowledged sickly as Luc's mouth came crushing down on hers. Anger corroded desire into a dark, stygian force. It burned, branded and destroyed it…

Carrie moaned deep in her throat as she felt her body overwhelm her self-control, overtaken by a vortex of hunger of such ferocity that it made her quake, spilling through her like lava, overwhelming everything in its path.

She was no longer Carrie, the calm, cool, logical woman she knew; she had become another Carrie—a Carrie who wanted nothing more than to feast on the hot pressure of Luc's mouth, to feel nothing but the touch of his hands on her body, doing what they were doing right now, shaping her curves, skimming her breasts with rough urgency and then returning to caress them with the knowing, urgent touch of an impatient lover.

There was no finesse between them, no delicate, hesitant or exploratory touching, just a white-hot explosion of searing need that had been dammed up for far too long.

Carrie sobbed with longing as Luc thrust one leg between her own, leaning heavily into her so that she could feel every taut inch of him pulsing hard against her body.

Deep inside herself she could feel her own responsive melting heat, and then Luc's hand was pushing aside the top of her gown, his fingers splaying against her near naked breast. Carrie shuddered, already imagining the sensation of his tongue against her nipple, and then his mouth, its soft, rough suck, whilst he—

A burst of laughter and music as other guests opened the salon doors brought Carrie back to reality with a sharply slicing stab.

Luc had released her mouth and was also releasing her, she recognised.

'Luc! I've been looking everywhere for you!' Another guest called out from across the deck.

Carrie's hands shook as she adjusted the front of her dress. Refusing to even look at Luc, she turned away from him to stare out into the darkness of the sea.

Her whole body felt cold and heavy. The knowledge of what she had done nauseated her. If she could have done so she would have walked past Luc and kept on walking until she was safely over S'Antander's border. But she had Harry to think of. Luc would not hesitate to ruin her brother if she did not do as he wished. She knew that!

To Carrie's relief the evening had finally come to an end. Her cheekbones ached from smiling, the backs of her eyes felt hot and dry, and she hated Luc more than she had thought it would ever be possible for one human being to hate another!

Having followed her back into the yacht's main salon, he had kept her closely pinioned to his side for the rest of the evening—wearing her, she had decided contemptuously, like a public declaration of intent.

Carrie had not been surprised when, after three failed attempts to detach him from her, Gina had made a very theatrical departure, entwined around a hunky young man who, Carrie had heard another guest whispering, was an up-and-coming young actor.

'There is such a thing as over-egging the bread, Luc,' Carrie had warned him pithily at one point.

'Meaning?' he had challenged her immediately.

'Meaning that it seems rather pointless to keep me physically shackled to your side, as though we are joined at the hip, when most of the other guests here have either already seen you tonight with Gina, looking anything but a newly betrothed man, or know perfectly well that you and Gina are lovers. Probably both!'

'My relationship with Gina—' Luc had stopped sharply, with a frown.

'Is no business of mine?' Carrie had finished sleekly for him. 'No, I am delighted to say that it isn't, since you don't mean anything to me any more,' she had continued.

It had given her a real sense of triumph and confidence to be able to say such a thing to him—especially after what had happened up on deck!

Now they were inside the car she deliberately sat as far away from Luc as she could, keeping her face turned towards the window as she gazed silently through it.

As the car climbed up the zigzagging road that led to the castle she could see the twinkling lights of the harbour below them.

'If you want the driver to make a detour to Gina's villa, don't feel inhibited because of me,' she taunted Luc, withdrawing her gaze from the view and turning to look at him. 'Or is that not the done thing?' she mocked him. 'No doubt you prefer to slip out of the castle unnoticed and—'

'I have already told you—the relationship between myself and Gina—'

'Is none of my business. I know,' Carrie agreed coolly.

She really was beginning to feel quite proud of herself. She wasn't a masochist—far from it—so she wasn't trying to inflict pain on herself by talking about Luc's lover; no, what she was doing was simply reminding herself, reinforcing to herself, what kind of man Luc actually was so that she could totally demolish that odd and disturbing feeling she had experienced in his arms!

A timely reminder to herself now was a very judicious move for self-protection, she assured herself, and if Luc did not like what she was saying—which he quite plainly did not, to judge from the angry glitter she could see in his eyes and the hard look to his mouth—then that was just too bad!

As they drove in under the gatehouse of what had been the original fortified castle, the two sentries on duty saluted.

The limousine purred to a halt, not outside the huge imposing main entrance to the castle but instead at the more discreet double doors that led to Luc's private apartments.

Luc accompanied her in grim silence to the doors, which were opened as though by magic at their approach by two white-gloved footmen.

The waiting major-domo bowed them in, and although none of them was wearing their uniforms the effect was still one of immense formality.

The private apartments of S'Antander's ruler had been created at the same time as the Hapsburg family had run riot through their many European palaces with baroque rococo interiors, and was very much of that era.

Luc had once ruefully commented to Carrie that he sometimes longed to look up at a ceiling that wasn't plastered, frescoed and gilded to within an inch of its life—to one that was simply instead a smooth white ceiling.

Carrie remembered how shocked she had been at the time, that Luc should make such a statement about such obviously historic and beautiful surroundings, but now she could see how he might long for the simplicity and starkness of a modern minimalist interior—rather in the way that simple bread and cheese is longed for after a surfeit of rich food.

If one was really in love with and loved by a man like Luc, the almost constant physical presence of other people, never mind their constant attendance, would be an unwanted intrusion on one's longed for intimacy, Carrie suspected. But so far as she was concerned right now she was only too glad of the fact that other people were around.

In another time, another world, she might have dreamed longingly of Luc drawing her gently into the shadows afforded by the long corridors and flights of stairs in order to kiss her passionately, too hungry for her to wait until they were in the secluded privacy of a shared room, but of course now that was the last thing she wanted to happen!

'I'll leave you here,' Luc announced tersely as they reached the point where the stairs branched out in two different directions.

As befitted a merely betrothed young woman she was in a suite at the opposite end of the private apartments to Luc.

Disconcertingly, as though he had looked into her head

and read her mind, Luc added curtly, 'Obviously once we are married we shall be sharing the master suite which was originally my grandparents' and then my parents'.'

Sharing? Carrie's whole body clenched and her heart somersaulted fiercely.

Again, as though he had guessed her thoughts, he continued, 'Under the circumstances we shall, of course, be occupying separate bedrooms.' He gave a small shrug. 'Since S'Antander is already behind the times in many ways, the fact that we are in separate rooms will not appear unusual or worthy of comment. Naturally,' he added sternly, 'only you and I will be aware that once we are alone the communicating doors between the two rooms will not be allowed to stand open but will be firmly closed.'

With that he turned on his heel and started to walk away from her, leaving her to stare after his retreating back whilst she battled with a very complex mix of emotions.

His statement about their sleeping arrangements, which should have made her feel relieved, had in fact given rise to other, deeper and very worrying feelings.

If she was honest she was suffering from a sharp pang of rejection so strong that it was overwhelming everything else she should have been feeling.

Even though physically she was tired, her mind would not allow her to go to sleep, so she changed out of her full-length dress into a much more relaxed outfit, and all the while re-ran what had happened, frantically seeking different ways she might have dealt with events which would have allowed her to walk free instead of becoming trapped in such an unwanted and potentially very dangerous situation.

And it *was* a dangerous situation, Carrie admitted unhappily. Emotionally, mentally and with every instinct of self-preservation and intelligence she possessed she knew she had every right to loathe and detest Luc. But physically her body was refusing to fall into line. Her body, to put it in its simplest form, was still very, very aware of Luc as a man; sexually she was still responsive to him, she admitted grimly.

If it had been just a matter of putting up with a marriage of convenience to him for a few months to protect and save her brother she could have gritted her teeth and got on with it, she was sure, but the potential complications of her unwanted physical response to Luc changed everything.

She would have to talk to Luc, she decided in panic. She would have to tell him that she had changed her mind! If necessary she'd beg him not to do anything to harm Harry!

Although it was almost midnight she knew that Luc favoured late nights and even early-morning hours in which to catch up with his paperwork, working in a room off his bedroom which he had had turned into a private office.

Impelled by a sense of urgency she couldn't ignore, Carrie opened her bedroom door and hurried down the corridor.

Outside Luc's door she hesitated only briefly, and then, taking a deep breath, she knocked on the door.

CHAPTER SIX

CARRIE began to frown when there was no response to her knock. Perhaps... She tensed as the door suddenly opened and she saw Luc glaring down at her. His hair was still damp from the shower he had obviously been taking when she had knocked on the door, to judge from the small rivulet of water she could see running from the hollow of his throat down over the slick, fine hair covering his chest before disappearing into the deep vee of the white towelling robe he had pulled on.

'Carrie!'

To cover what she was feeling, Carrie returned sharply, 'Who did you think it was? Gina?' giving a small outraged gasp as a lean hand shot out to manacle her wrist and virtually drag her into the room.

'There's something I want to say to you Luc,' Carrie began as he pushed the door closed, trapping them both in the privacy of his bedroom.

He smelled of soap and clean male flesh and... To her shame Carrie realised that she was actually closing her eyes—all the better to savour the pheromone-drenched warm air that surrounded him.

'What now?' he demanded sardonically. 'Couldn't it have waited until morning?'

'No, it could not,' Carrie retorted, welcoming the rescuing anger his attitude was arousing inside her.

There was a small and decidedly hostile silence whilst he looked at her.

'I don't know why on earth you insist on forcing me

to marry you, Luc, when you've got a ready-made and far more suitable potential bride who just can't wait to get her hands on you in the shape of your lover—Gina!'

Carrie felt herself begin to tremble inwardly as she heard the feverish intensity in her own voice.

Luc's eyes had narrowed and his whole attention was concentrated on her There was an ominous look in them which made Carrie realise she had gone too far, but recklessly she refused to heed it.

'She wants you, Luc,' she told him. 'And I don't. And—'

'Look, Carrie I can see you're spoiling for an argument, but let me warn you right now I'm not in the best of moods myself. If you continue to goad me the way you're doing right now—well, I just hope that you're prepared to meet the consequences,' Luc interrupted her sharply.

'If by "the consequences" you mean that you'll pull every trick you can to stop me winning it—' Carrie began furiously,

'No.' Luc silenced her. 'The consequence I was referring to is the physical fall-out we seem to generate between us every time you push me to the limit. And right now you are perilously close to that limit. There is something about you, Carrie, that drives me to the point when I am so incensed, so insane with fury, that— Oh, forget it,' he told her curtly, releasing her wrist and stepping back from her.

'Forget it?' As she rubbed her wrist Carrie glared at him. 'Oh, that's typical of you, isn't it? You insult me and then you tell me to forget it. We aren't all quite as good at conveniently forgetting things as you, Luc...'

'What the hell is that supposed to mean,' he demanded harshly.

When she didn't reply his mouth hardened.

'I wish to God you'd washed that damned perfume off your skin before you came in here.'

Carrie stared at him.

'There's nothing wrong with my perfume,' she defended herself immediately. 'It's the same one I've always worn...'

'Yes, I know that, damn you,' Luc ground out.

'And for your information,' she continued, 'quite a lot of people have complimented me on it and said how much it suits me.'

'I'm sure they have—especially if by "other people" you mean other men! God, Carrie, you certainly know how to push all the wrong buttons where I'm concerned.'

'Well, the feeling is certainly mutual,' Carrie snapped back immediately.

'It is?'

The look he gave her jolted against her nerve-endings like an electric charge, but she was too angry to heed its warning.

'Because right now there is nothing, but nothing, I'd like more to exorcise what you've driven me to, Carrie—in the only way it can be exorcised!'

She was still battling to understand his enigmatic and foreboding statement when he started to move towards her.

'Luc!' she protested in instinctive self-protection and denial, her stomach muscles cramping as she suddenly recognised the angry arousal surrounding him like a force field. The energy of his passion was engulfing her as well, she acknowledged weakly, and her own body started to respond to the hotly sexual messages his was giving off.

As he reached for her she told herself that she would protest, struggle, resist the insane pull of her own self-destructive longing, but instead the moment his arms tightened around her she could feel herself melting into him, shivering with sharp stabs of excited, aching need as her hands tugged feverishly at his robe so that she could move even closer to his naked body.

'No, you haven't changed,' she heard him muttering thickly. 'You still do things to me that no woman has any right to be able to do to a man. And there have been so many men for you, haven't there, Carrie?'

Carrie could feel his anger, hear it in his voice, but her own desire was cushioning her from it, distancing her from it. Her fingers touched his bare skin and desire ran through her like sheet lightning.

'Luc!' His name was a paper-thin whisper, torn raggedly from her aching throat as she pressed her lips to the line of his shoulder, intoxicated by the warm, salty male taste of him, the manly feel of him. Eagerly she ran her fingertips along his skin, enjoying the sensation of the taut muscles clenching whilst she kissed her way up his throat and along his jaw. She relished the sexily slightly rough stubble against the smoothness of her mouth. With her fingertips she traced the shape of his lips, pressing them wantonly against them as she held his gaze.

Sensuously and slowly she caressed his lips, shuddering when he finally opened them, seizing on her wrist so that she could not move her hand and then sucking slowly and deliberately on her fingers.

How could such a simple action have such a powerful effect? Carrie could almost feel her womb contracting in the most urgently sexual way as her body registered its reaction to him.

Luc had released her fingers and was guiding her hand down his body. Carrie shuddered again violently as she felt the hard fullness of his arousal, and her fingers opened hungrily over his taut flesh, to enclose it with a fierce thrill of remembered passionate pleasure.

As a teenager she had been awed and half shocked to discover that she could not close her hand fully around him, but now that knowledge sent a message of intense female delight to her body rather than one of nervous hesitation.

Her own wantonness shocked Carrie, but her responsiveness to him was beyond her control—a freak of nature too wild and untameable to be set within normal known boundaries.

That part of her that she had always resisted acknowledging or knowing was glorying openly in what was happening, revelling in Luc's nudity and her own access to him; it was even urging her to tear off her own clothes so that she could be as physically close to him as it was possible to be—skin to skin, body on body, flesh within flesh... Or, better still, an inner voice urged her, incite Luc to remove them for her... Her body contracted violently with fierce pleasure, her mouth opening eagerly for the thrust of Luc's tongue, and she bent his head to take it into her possession, melding them together with a kiss that was a maelstrom of dangerously dark emotions.

The intimacy they were sharing was their battleground, Carrie recognised, and on it they were both intent on destroying their shared past and one another. But, even knowing that, she could not bear to stop. She was being driven by an urgency, a compulsion that could not be stopped.

She felt Luc tugging at her clothes, impatiently jerking down the zip of her top and then pushing it aside to explore her naked torso.

His hand shaped the breasts she so eagerly and fiercely offered to him, their softness filling his hands as he held and moulded their full curves, the small circular movement of his thumbs against their taut crests driving her mad with longing, making her press herself even more urgently against him.

She was trembling helplessly from head to foot in her longing to feel the deep, slow suckle of his mouth against the swollen longing of her nipples, to feel the shockingly erotic graze of his teeth, to feel…

Carrie heard herself moan when Luc removed his hand from her breast to slide one arm behind her to support her before bending her back over it.

The heat she could see in his eyes as he gazed down at her naked breasts was enough to set tinder alight, she acknowledged giddily as he lifted her towards his mouth and started slowly caressing one pleadingly erect peak.

If pleasure could ever be described in terms of colour, then hers was shot through with every shade of the rainbow and then some, Carrie admitted helplessly, her whole body alive with sensation and need as it gave itself up to Luc's sensual domination.

From her breasts his mouth moved to the valley between them, and began a slow, unhurried descent that involved his tongue describing tormenting circles of pleasure of ever-increasing intensity.

Carrie felt him lower her feet back to the ground and move his hands to span her waist. He knelt on the floor, the downward movement of his lips not stopping until they reached the low-slung waistband of her velour pants.

Violent shudders racked her; her hands clutched at his shoulders, her nails unwittingly digging into his flesh. She felt him pause and then begin to tug down her pants and underwear.

The soft feathering of hair covering her sex could not

disguise the tempting, pouting arousal of her body as it flaunted its longing for him

With every kiss that took him closer to the sexual core of her Carrie could feel her heart slamming with increasing ferocity against her ribs.

She was blind, deaf—oblivious to everything but her own need and the huge dammed-up forbidden force of it she had hidden in denial for so very long.

This was why no other man had ever come anywhere near to interesting her enough to share anything more than a mere dinner date with him; this was why she had had found it so easy to live the life of a nun. This…and Luc. Luc…Luc…

Carrie only realised that she was sobbing his name aloud when the deliberate, delicate movement of his tongue against her sex suddenly became the white-hot pressure of his mouth, taking, possessing, exposing both of them in the true, intense ferocity of their mutual need.

The swift, spasming contractions of her pleasure came so quickly that she cried out against them, her fingers twining in Luc's dark hair as she sobbed out the earthy intensity of her release.

She could feel Luc easing his mouth away from her body and then lifting her, carrying her over to the huge bed, placing her in its centre and moving over her, into her.

The hot, full feel of him within her was a sensation that took her straight back to the past, to the aching sweetness of the innocent virginal surrender of herself to him.

This time too she was giving herself to him, to the increasingly urgent rhythm he was imposing on her willing flesh. She could feel the tiny tremors of sensual excitement starting to build up again, but they were different this time—deeper, stronger, holding him, drawing him fully within her body; she wanted him as close as he could get to where she most longed to have him.

She could feel the harshness of his breath as his own desire overtook him, each thrust of his body binding them closer, deepening the responsive quivers of her own.

Like an avalanche her climax thundered down on her, exploding inside her only a heartbeat after she felt Luc's hot release.

His heart was thudding heavily against her body, and she could still hear the sound of his laboured breathing.

As the unwanted emotion of what had happened finally flooded through her, filling her eyes with stinging tears, she heard Luc demanding savagely, 'What is it about you, Carrie, that drives a man to commit an act he can only despise himself for...?'

She could see the look of angry contempt in his eyes as he moved away from her and headed for the bathroom.

For a moment she felt too distressed and weak to move. Right now, more than anything else, she ached for the warmth and comfort of his arms, for his reassurance that he had not meant what he had said...

Shakily she got up off the bed and dragged on her clothes. All those years ago she had ached for those things too. She had not received them then and she certainly was not going to do so now! How much of a fool did she have to make of herself? Carrie wondered sickly as she headed for the bedroom door and pulled it open. Had she really not learned her lesson the first time around?

Carrie stared anxiously at her expression in the bedroom mirror. Did she look as puffy-eyed as she felt? Or had she managed to hide the effects of her nearly sleepless night with the make-up she had just applied? Certainly Benita, her maid, had not said anything when she had brought

Carrie her early-morning cup of tea and helped her to dress—other than to tell her excitedly that workmen were already beginning to decorate the town ready for the celebration of the country's Centenary and the Royal Wedding—her wedding to Luc!

Carrie tensed as she heard a very firm knock on her bedroom door. Her gaze fixed on it as it opened and Luc walked in.

Typically, he was dressed formally in an immaculate suit.

'Good—you're here,' he began curtly. 'Look, Carrie, about last night—'

'I don't want to talk about it.' She stopped him immediately, getting up and pacing the room as she tried to hide her distress and agitation. 'Just who did you think I was, Luc?' she demanded. 'Your mistress?'

She could barely endure to breathe the same air as him, never mind look at him. Even the silence between them made her raw nerve-endings flinch in pain.

'I behaved in a way that perhaps I should not have done. I admit that,' Luc acknowledged coolly. 'But I wasn't entirely to blame—was I, Carrie?'

Unable to stop herself or protect herself, she demanded, 'What do you mean?'

He was going to taunt her for her response to him. She knew that, but somehow she could not stop herself from inviting the humiliation and pain.

'You pushed me, Carrie. You goaded me and taunted me, and I reacted as any man would have.'

Carrie was too relieved to object to what he was saying.

'I warn you now that if you're expecting me to apologise to you—' Luc continued grimly.

Released from her fear, Carrie felt a surge of strengthening anger.

'What? You apologise to a mere nobody like me? Of course not! Perish the thought!' she agreed witheringly.

'One of the reasons I want to speak with you is that my godmother came to see me first thing this morning…'

'Did she? Well, I'm sure it wasn't to congratulate you on our betrothal!' Carrie murmured dryly.

She could see that Luc was frowning at her.

'Oh, come on, Luc,' she told him irritably. 'She hates the thought of me marrying you almost as much as I do.'

'Carrie—' he began grittily, and then stopped as they both heard the sudden barrage of noise that exploded outside the window.

'What the devil—?'

Carrie could see quite clearly where a plume of smoke was rising from the harbour.

'Stay here,' Luc ordered her tersely.

CHAPTER SEVEN

CARRIE walked restlessly along one of the paths of the beautifully designed private courtyard garden, going for the umpteenth time to stand by the wall and look through the open arched 'window' down to the harbour below.

It was over two hours since Luc had left. The whole castle was abuzz with speculation about the cause of the explosion which had been responsible for the noise they had all heard earlier—and apparently the destruction of one of the yachts in the marina—but no one seemed able to confirm exactly what had happened or why.

The garden—which, Carrie suspected, would normally have been a restful haven—felt like a restrictive prison. What was happening? Where was Luc? She was tempted to go down to the harbour herself, to find out what was going on. In fact she *would* go down to the harbour, Carrie decided determinedly, hurrying back into the castle.

She was just walking past the doors leading to a corridor that led to the area of the castle used for administrative and governmental offices when they opened and Luc came out.

There was a smudge of dirt across his forehead and what looked like a sooty mark spoiling the immaculate appearance of his suit.

'Luc?' Carrie demanded, standing in front of him. 'What's happening? They're saying that one of the yachts in the marina exploded.'

'Yes,' Luc agreed tersely.

Carrie went pale.

'Not Jay's?' she exclaimed anxiously.

Immediately Luc's mouth thinned. 'No, it was not my cousin's—although I am sure he will be delighted to know how concerned you are for him. In fact the yacht in question was fortunately unoccupied, although that does not negate the seriousness of the situation. I don't believe for one minute that the individuals who planted the bomb that caused the damage had any intention of actually injuring anyone, but—'

'A bomb?' Carrie's voice betrayed her shocked disbelief. 'Someone put a bomb on one of the yachts? But who on earth would do such a thing, here in S'Antander? This kind of behaviour can't be condoned by the majority of protestors. Their behaviour has always been peaceful until now, hasn't it?'

She was still shaking her head, unable to comprehend what had happened, when Jay himself came striding down the corridor towards them, announcing, 'I've only just heard the news. I had to fly out to a business meeting in Zurich this morning and I've only now got back. I suppose they hit on Zurafi's yacht because of all the bad press he's been getting lately—speculation about his involvement in arms dealing. I've got to warn you, Luc, there's one of a hell of a lot of worried noise coming from the international tax exile crowd. This has made them decidedly jittery. You and S'Antander are going to be in a vulnerable position if—'

'I do realise the danger, Jay.' Carrie heard Luc interrupt his cousin tersely. 'But right now there is very little I can do about it. Of course there are those who have made it plain that they favour having the perpetrators hunted down and flung in some convenient and highly unpleasant dungeon—and I realise that I must find those responsible and they must be punished for their crime—but of course that is exactly what these young idiots hope will happen. That way they would be turned into political martyrs overnight, instead of being seen as merely a bunch of idealistic troublemakers, and bring down the full wrath of the Human Rights Commission upon us. As if things weren't difficult enough…'

'So, what are you going to do?' Jay asked him.

When Luc made no response Jay exploded irritably.

'Oh, come on, Luc—you can't just let them get away with it.'

Luc's eyebrows rose.

'Okay, okay.' Jay backed off immediately, spreading his hands in a gesture of apology.

'You're the boss here, Luc. What you say goes!'

'In my grandfather's day that might have been true, but today…' Luc frowned and turned to look out of the window. He seemed very distracted, and, Carrie suspected, he had forgotten that she was even there.

'I'm booked on a flight for New York tonight,' Jay told him. 'I've got an urgent meeting I can't get out of. But if you need me, Luc, or if there's anything I can do…'

Carrie watched as the two men embraced. They really were amazingly alike, especially in profile, and to the casual observer might even have passed as twins.

After Jay had gone Luc turned to look at Carrie.

'I've made arrangements for you to be driven to Milan the day after tomorrow,' he told her flatly. 'You're going to need a suitable wedding dress, and it seems that only two designers can guarantee to have one made for you in time. Appointments have been made for you to attend their salons. I had intended to go with you myself, but under the circumstances…'

His high-handed attitude infuriated Carrie. But his

words also sent a juddering sense of anxiety knifing through her at the thought of their upcoming marriage.

'Of course you can't go now, Luc. You'll be far too busy bullying and terrifying these "activists". But then you like doing things like that, don't you? And, though their latest methods are unsound, has it occurred to you yet that they might have a point? That in some people's eyes, *you* are the one in the wrong? Some people—decent, right-thinking people—would be appalled and…and disgusted at the thought of a ruler who supports and protects people who have acquired their wealth in the ways those exiles they are protesting against have done. But then you don't care what other people think or feel, do you Luc? You never have and you ever will.'

'That's enough.'

The harsh sound of Luc's voice brought her outburst to trembling silence.

'For your information,' Luc continued, but stopped speaking as the double doors burst open and an agitated aide hurried up to him.

'Highness—there has been a communication from… from the activists. It is addressed to you…'

'Give it to me,' Luc commanded him grimly.

Carrie watched tensely as he opened and then read the missive he had been handed.

'What does it say?' she asked.

For a moment she thought he was going to refuse to reply, but after dismissing the hovering aide he said curtly, 'It says that the bombings will continue until I agree to meet their terms.'

'Their terms…?'

Before she could get any further the doors opened again, this time to admit several of the senior members of the council, one of whom demanded tersely, 'Highness—

is it true? Have they actually dared to make demands? My God, in your grandfather's day they would have lost their liberty for such an outrage. He would never have tolerated such actions. Treasonable actions, Luc, which by rights—'

'Henri, calm down. Otherwise you will cause yourself a second heart attack,' Carrie heard Luc caution the older man dryly.

'What about the fifth Centenary celebrations and your marriage, Highness?' another official was asking anxiously. 'Ought they to be cancelled? Will it be safe?'

Carrie held her breath. Was she going to be allowed to escape from the situation Luc had forced her into after all?

Silently she prayed that she might be, but to her disappointment Luc refused to answer the question outright, saying calmly instead, 'We already know that there are serious and complex questions at issue here, and because of that I intend to call a full council meeting. In the meantime the public and our people need to be reassured that they are safe, and to that end I shall give orders that those activists who are known to us are to be taken into custody.'

CHAPTER EIGHT

CARRIE couldn't believe just how quickly the last three weeks had passed. She had been kept busy with a plethora of appointments and minor semi-official functions, all of which she had had to attend without Luc, since he had been out of the country for most of this time on matters of state business.

But now he was back for their wedding!

She gave a small shudder. She didn't want to think about the number of hours she had wasted thinking about him, and she certainly did not want to admit to the amount of sleep she had lost, not just thinking about him but... Determinedly she switched her thoughts away from her own emotions to concentrate instead on those of her maid.

Benita was most definitely not herself!

'Is something wrong, Benita?' Carrie asked her maid sympathetically, whilst she waited for Benita to help her to dress for the formal dinner Luc was giving that evening. She hadn't seen him all week, and the last time she *had* seen him they had quarrelled again, with her coming off worst. She had thought about refusing to attend tonight's dinner, but warily she recognised that Luc was fully capable of storming her bedroom and dressing her himself, if he saw fit!

'You look very pale,' she told her maid in concern. 'Aren't you feeling well?'

To Carrie's dismay the maid's eyes brimmed with huge tears, whilst the lips she had pressed firmly together in an effort to control her emotions began to tremble.

'Benita!' Carrie protested. 'What's wrong?'

'Nothing… It… I…' Benita shook her head, fighting for self-control, but her emotions overwhelmed her. 'It is my cousin,' she wept. 'He has been taken into custody by the authorities. They suspect him of being…of… He did not mean any harm. He just believes—' She stopped. 'He is only sixteen, and his mother—my aunt—is a widow. I am so afraid for him…'

Fresh tears filled her eyes, and Carrie, with a vulnerable brother of her own to worry about, ached with sympathy and understanding for her.

'We had no idea that he was involved—' Benita broke off again, and bit her lip. 'We cannot find out where he is, and we have not been allowed to speak with him. It has been over two weeks since he was arrested and my aunt is beside herself…'

It was too much for Carrie to bear.

'Benita, why on earth didn't you say something before? What is his name?' she asked impetuously. 'I shall speak to L—to his Highness and try to find out where he is for you.'

Immediately the other girl's face was wreathed in a sparkling smile of gratitude, whilst Carrie realised sinkingly what she had done. It was too late for her to regret her impetuosity now though!

Carrie had chosen her outfit for the dinner carefully, fully prepared to do for her maid's sake what she would never have dreamed of doing for her own—and that was create the right impression to placate Luc and hopefully put him in the kind of mood where he would be open to an appeal on behalf of Benita's young cousin.

Her admirable intentions lasted just as long as it took

her to discover that the Countess was one of the dinner guests!

Carrie had barely had time to do more than take a sip of her pre-dinner cocktail before the Countess swept up to Luc, her lips pursing disapprovingly as she glared at Carrie.

'So, Luc,' she began, 'what is to be done about this disgraceful business? You will have to cancel the wedding now, of course, and the Fifth Centenary celebrations! It simply will not be safe. How can we invite foreign dignitaries to our country when at any moment they could be blown apart by these dangerous criminals who seem so determined to destroy everything your grandfather worked for?'

Before Carrie could stop herself she heard herself protesting hotly. 'While I firmly oppose some of their methods, I strongly believe that the majority of these activists are not criminals; they are simply a group of people who have ideals and moral beliefs! And quite frankly—'

'What? You *support* them?' The Countess stopped her furiously. 'Luc, have you heard this?' she exclaimed. 'Mind you, I suppose it is only to be expected. You see how unfit she is to be your wife?' she demanded, her mouth thinning. 'As a member of the ruling class of this country, Luc, I can only deplore what is happening. But as your godmother,' she added mock piously, 'I must say I am relieved that this shocking event has revealed just how impossible it is for you to marry this…this person. The wedding will have to be cancelled immediately, and an announcement made to the effect that your betrothal is at an end.'

The look Luc gave Carrie could have shredded glass, she recognised warily as he turned the full force of his

disapproving, hard-eyed stare on her before turning back
to his godmother.

Well, at least she would have her freedom, Carrie acknowledged hollowly, even though she was gaining it at
the hands of a woman she loathed. She could hear the bite
of the anger Luc has just shown her in his voice when he
replied.

'I appreciate your concern, Godmother, but I am afraid
that the wedding cannot and will not be cancelled. The
celebrations and the marriage will both take place,' Luc
continued curtly, ignoring the anger and disbelief on the
faces of both the women looking at him.

'The last thing this country needs now is the kind of
panic that will ensue if either event is cancelled. In fact,
if anything, it is even more important than ever that they
do take place!'

'I realise that you do not particularly like my godmother,
Carrie, but it was hardly diplomatic of you to speak to
her the way you did earlier this evening.'

Carrie gave Luc a bitterly hostile look. The dinner was
over and the guests had departed. She and Luc were alone
in the Green Salon and Carrie had just been on the point
of making her escape when Luc had started to speak.

'If you want my opinion she doesn't deserve to be
treated with diplomacy,' Carrie told him with asperity. 'I
have every right to my own opinions, Luc, and I'm not
changing them for you or anyone else. You might be able
to force me to marry you, but there's no way you can
force me to change the way I think or feel!'

'Did I say I wanted to?'

The silky comment took her aback.

'Well, you certainly want to change everything else

about me,' she retorted quickly, plucking at the skirt of her dress as she added disparagingly, 'My clothes, my—'

'Your temper?' Luc offered sardonically. 'Your incredible stubbornness? Yes, I would certainly like to see those moderated a little, shall we say, but there are other aspects of your personality that I have to admit are admirable.'

Carrie stared at him. Praise from Luc—and for her? This was the last thing she had expected.

Warily she looked at him.

'What aspects?' she demanded suspiciously.

Luc shot her a brief look she could not analyse before responding dispassionately, 'Your defence of the underdog, your championing of moral causes, your compassion for those less fortunate than yourself,' he told her promptly.

Open-mouthed Carrie blinked. Luc actually *liked* something about her? Approved of and valued things about her?

Her sense of giddy pleasure was swiftly squashed as Luc added coolly, 'These are excellent attributes in the consort of a man in my position. A wife with what used to be called ''the common touch'' is an invaluable asset when one—'

'I am not going to be your ''consort'' or your wife,' she told him bitingly. 'I am merely going to be the woman you marry!'

Immediately his eyebrows rose.

'There's a difference,' he asked her dryly.

Carrie wasn't going to be taunted into backing down.

'Yes. There is!' she said fiercely. 'A woman you marry is just that. But a *wife* is…'

As she saw the way Luc was looking at her she stopped mid-speech, her face overheating.

'You know what I mean,' she muttered angrily. 'Anyway, there's something I need to…to ask you, Luc,' she told him. The conversation was getting out of control, and she was anxious to escape to her own room, but first there was her promise to her maid!

A little breathlessly, she told him what Benita had said to her.

'And what is it, exactly, you are expecting me to do?' he demanded scathingly. 'Command his release just because his cousin is your maid? Despite what you think, Carrie, my powers are not omnipotent. We have laws in this country which have to be upheld!'

'He's only sixteen,' Carrie told him stubbornly. 'His family do not even know where he is and have not been allowed to speak with him. You say you have laws, Luc? Well, every right-thinking modern country has laws that preclude them from locking up sixteen-year-olds without telling their families…or at least they should have. What is happening here is tantamount to an abuse of people's human rights, and if you want my opinion that fact should be made public. In fact, if I were a journalist and not an economist…'

She stopped speaking as he looked at her.

'If that is a threat, Carrie…' he said pleasantly.

Carrie had had enough.

'Oh, I see—it's all right for you to threaten, bully and blackmail me, is it? But the moment you think *you* are the one who might be forced into doing something you turn all moralistic—even through you are the one who is in the wrong—'

'There is far more involved here than a mere personal vendetta,' Luc interrupted her curtly. 'There are issues at stake here, Carrie, of far-reaching importance. Issues of far more consequence than either you or I.'

Stubbornly Carrie refused to say anything.

She heard Luc draw in his breath in what might have been either a sigh of irritation or one of resignation.

'Very well,' he agreed grimly. 'What is this young man's name? You may inform your maid that I shall do my best to find out where he is and make sure that his family are informed. But that is all I will do, Carrie!'

Exhaling a little shakily, Carrie gave him Benita's cousin's name.

'And in return for this favour I am to do for you,' Luc continued smoothly, 'what, may I ask, do you intend to do for me? Historically, of course—at least if one is to believe Hollywood—there is only one method of payment, one form of currency between a man and woman under such circumstances. So what is this young man's freedom worth to you, Carrie? One night in my bed? Two?'

Carrie stared at him in disbelief.

'You don't mean that!' she insisted feebly.

A cynical look shadowed his face.

'Hardly. After all, I know how worthless a reward it is, don't I? Since you have given it—and yourself—to so many others already!'

CHAPTER NINE

LUC replaced the telephone receiver into which he had been speaking and walked over to the window of his private office. From it he could look down into the courtyard below, where Carrie was pacing one of the ornamental gravel pathways. She had, as Luc knew, just finished having the final fitting of her wedding gown, and the movement of her body reminded him of an angry feline, all pent-up heat and energy.

His telephone call had been to an old friend and very distant family connection whose input he had been seeking with regard to the situation confronting him.

'Tough one, Luc,' his third cousin four times removed or thereabouts had informed him cheerfully. 'From the looks of it you're well and truly in a "damned if you do and damned if you don't" situation, so to speak! I know that privately you sympathise with the feelings of the activists, even if you can't say so publicly. But unfortunately, from what you've hinted to me, you've got some real nasties left over from your grandfather's day tucked away in S'Antander's vaults, who aren't going to take kindly to being evicted and are potentially one hell of a lot more dangerous than those insurgents of yours!'

'Tell me about it,' Luc had agreed feelingly.

His cousin had laughed.

'I hear you're still going ahead with the Fifth Centenary celebrations and the wedding. I'm not sure I would want to. I know S'Antander is a small state, but policing that kind of affair... It would only take one suicide bomber!'

Both of them had fallen silent before Luc had answered dryly, 'Thanks!'

'My money's on you, Luc,' his cousin had assured him. 'Knowing you, you'll find a way of dealing with the situation.'

As he recalled his relative's rueful words now, Luc's expression darkened slightly and he continued to watch Carrie. The fiery passion which was so much a part of her personality was plain to see in her reaction to her situation.

Like all young men he had once dreamed idealistic, unattainable dreams, and Carrie had… The intrusion of unwanted thoughts and memories made him frown. Didn't he already have enough to concern and occupy him? Hadn't those stern guardians who had brought him up made sure that they instilled into him that he was a ruler first and a man second?

Carrie's head ached. She was sick of hearing her maid singing Luc's praises for having the compassion and the forbearance to put all the activists under house arrest, rather than keeping them in prison, and she was sick, too, of hearing people blather on ceaselessly about the wedding—as though it were something she was supposed to be looking forward to and not a punishment that was being forced upon her, Carrie thought furiously as she paced the private courtyard garden.

She had spent virtually all morning being prodded and pinned beneath the critical eye of the designers from the couture house who'd agreed to rush through the making of her wedding gown, and gowns for the ten attendants she was apparently going to be having. And this afternoon a hairstylist and make-up artist were coming to do a run-through prior to the dress rehearsal for the wedding.

The wedding. Edgily Carrie pushed her hair off her face. In three days' time she and Luc were going to be married.

Every night she prayed that something would happen to set her free, and every morning she woke up to the realisation that her prayers were not likely to be answered.

The whole state seemed to be in an excited ferment already, in preparation for the celebration of the Fifth Centenary and the wedding. Only this morning Benita had happily told her that virtually everyone she knew was either throwing or going to a party in anticipation of the double event.

'What? Even the activists?' Carrie had queried dryly.

'Oh, yes.' Benita had responded blithely, before flushing and looking a little uncomfortable. 'It is only true that they do not agree with *some* of our country's current policies...' she had admitted.

Carrie had lifted one eyebrow, but said nothing.

'Well, only three days to go before you become a Serene Highness.'

The teasing voice of Luc's cousin made Carrie spin round, her face breaking into a warm smile as she welcomed him and returned his hug.

'Jay!' she exclaimed. 'When did you get back? I thought you were still in New York.'

'I flew into Nice this morning,' he told her. 'I was just on my way to see Luc when I spotted you out here. You've lost weight! Don't go getting too thin! A man likes a woman who feels like a woman! Mind you, when that woman is you...' He paused and shook his head. 'Luc is one hell of a lucky guy.'

'Flatterer.' Carrie laughed. They might look so physically alike that at a distance it was virtually impossible to tell them apart, but her body knew the difference between them. To her body Jay was a man who was a friend, but Luc… Her body responded to Luc in a way it had never ever done to any other man! Never had done, and never would do?

As she watched Jay hurrying off to see Luc, Carrie acknowledged the unwanted truth she had been fighting to deny ever since the night Luc had taken her to bed and in doing so had exploded the carefully constructed defences she had spent the years they had been apart maintaining.

She desired Luc…wanted him, ached for him, needed him in a way that was far too intense ever to be merely physical. There! She had made herself think the unthinkable. She had made herself recognise it and acknowledge it. She still loved Luc! And he still loathed her!

'So you're still going ahead with everything, then?'

As he faced his cousin across the polished expanse of his desk Luc nodded his head tersely.

'I don't have any other option,' Luc told him. 'The activists have delivered an ultimatum. Either I outlaw those who hold accounts here they do not approve of, or I abdicate!'

Jay let out a silent whistle. 'They've dared to make that kind of a challenge? I hadn't realised things had gone so far!'

'The situation has escalated faster than I expected myself,' Luc acknowledged. 'I could be wrong, but I am beginning to suspect that they are receiving backing—financial and political—from a third party—someone who perhaps has their own reason for wanting to see me step down. That would certainly explain why we are suddenly faced with terrorist tactics as opposed to peaceful, if vocal, demonstrations.'

As he spoke Luc gave Jay a coolly level look.

'Mmm… Well, I haven't heard anything on the international grapevine. I just saw Carrie outside,' he commented, changing the subject. 'Does she know yet what's going down?'

'No,' Luc responded tersely. 'And I don't intend that she will. I've set up some private meetings away from S'Antander to see if a diplomatic, behind the scenes solution can be found.'

'And if it can't?' Jay pressed him.

When Luc didn't answer him, he said, 'I'll tell you straight, Luc, this country is going to lose one hell of a lot of revenue if things don't improve. With the commitment you've made to provide improved schooling and medical care you just can't afford that.'

'Spare me the lectures, Jay,' Luc responded sharply.

'Oh, I nearly forgot. Gina asked me to give you a message,' Jay told him.

Luc frowned.

'I've already spoken with her.'

'And?'

A sharp look darkened Luc's eyes, making it plain that he did not relish his cousin's question.

'She has been offered a prestigious role in an upcoming movie. I've told her that she should take it. She's leaving S'Antander this evening.'

'You can be a ruthless bastard when you need to be, can't you?' Jay commented lightly.

Luc made no response. He saw no reason to inform his cousin that the 'affair' he was supposed to have shared with the actress had been little more than a publicity stunt conjured up by her to gain press attention. At the time it had suited him to go along with her pretence, and it had even amused him, in an ironic sort of way, to recognise that his betrothal had had the effect of making Gina behave as though they had in actual fact been lovers. Certainly she had played the role of abandoned and outraged lover with melodramatic enthusiasm, and he had had his own reasons for allowing her to do so! But she was the complete opposite of everything he found desirable in a woman.

Everything he found desirable! Automatically he walked over to the window and looked down into the courtyard.

Carrie had gone and it was empty. As he dropped his lashes to conceal his expression Luc was glad that only he was aware of the symbolism of those words, and just how much they had haunted his life.

Carrie had just walked into the Green Salon when her mobile rang. Recognising that the caller was her brother, she hesitated for a second before answering. There was no way she wanted to spoil Harry and Maria's happiness by telling them what had happened and how she was being blackmailed into marriage by Luc.

Taking a deep breath, she forced herself to smile as she said her brother's name.

'Carrie, you'll never guess what!' Harry burst into excited speech. 'Whilst Maria and I have been on honeymoon we've been doing some serious talking, and—well, to cut a long story short I'm going to give up my job in the City and Maria and I are going to look round for a farm to buy! You know how I've always wanted to.'

Carrie knew that this was true, but even so...

'Harry?' She stopped him cautiously. 'I understand

what you're saying—but the cost! You don't have any money, and—'

'Oh, we don't need to worry about that. Maria has a huge trust fund from her parents.' An indulgent, adoring note entered his voice as he added, 'Sensible girl—she's never let on to anyone because she didn't want to have any wastrel fortune-hunters chasing after her. God, Carrie I can't tell you how it feels to know I can pack in that wretched job. I never liked it; you know that!

'It all came out whilst we were away. Maria guessed that I was worrying about something, and when I told her—well, if I hadn't already been madly in love with her… She was just so sweet and understanding. She said she'd never liked the ideas of me working in the City anyway. She wants a family—and as soon as possible— we both do—so we're going to look round for the right place. Dad got in contact the other day, by the way. He and Liz are on a trip into the Outback, apparently, and they'll be gone for weeks. Where are *you*?'

Carrie opened her mouth to speak and found that she had to clear her throat before she could do so. 'I…'

'You're working,' Harry guessed. 'Okay, I'll keep it short—oh, but, Carrie—I'm just over the moon. Maria has turned my life around. Loving her, marrying her… You know better than anyone that the bank thing just wasn't working out for me, and I'd have come totally unstuck without your constant guidance. I'm not like you and Dad… I suppose I must be more like Ma—her family were farming stock, weren't they? Oh, Maria says—Oh, damn—we're breaking up. My battery's running down. Love and kisses, sis…'

As her brother's voice disappeared in a burst of staccato crackling followed by silence Carrie stared at her mobile. She was, she discovered with admirably detached interest, trembling from head to foot. With relief, of course. Relief because now she did not have to marry Luc! He no longer had the power to hurt Harry. He could still ruin *her* professionally, of course, but she could retrain—in a different field. She was still young enough, and surely anything was better than being forced into an unwanted marriage? And a lifetime of misery! She could just walk away right now. Right now this very minute…this very second…

Carrie was still contemplating the consequences of what she had just learned when she saw the Countess walking towards her.

'Where is Luc?' she demanded imperiously. 'I need to speak with him immediately.'

Carrie looked coolly back at her, her chin lifting determinedly.

'I'm afraid I don't know, and even if I did—' Carrie took a deep breath, reminding herself that she wasn't eighteen any more. Calmly and pointedly she went on, asking Maria's grandmother, 'Has anyone ever told you, I wonder, how very unpleasant and overbearing towards other people you are? Or, like all bullies, do you rely on the fact that people are too afraid of you to stand up to you?'

For several seconds all the Countess could do was stare at Carrie in disbelieving fury.

'I knew it!' she exclaimed at last, when she had mastered her shock. 'I knew all along just what you were. No decent, well brought up young woman would ever speak to one of her elders as you have just spoken to me! You obviously think that your position as Luc's fiancée is unassailable, but let me tell you that when Luc learns what I have to tell him about you he will never make you his wife!'

She gave Carrie a tight-lipped look of triumph. 'You

cannot know how much satisfaction it gives me to know that my suspicions about you have proved to be correct! It has taken a lot of persistence and a lot of money to unearth the truth. No doubt you thought it was safely buried, and that no one would ever know what you had done, but I have found you out!'

A tiny, icy finger of dread stroked a deathly chill along Carrie's spine.

'Nothing to say?' the Countess taunted her. 'Well, I am sure that Luc will have plenty of things he wants to say once I have apprised him of certain facts about you!'

The older woman's eyes were glittering with triumph and a malice that caused Carrie to feel acutely sick as the full horror of what she was going to have to face hit her.

Feigning an indifference she was fighting to protect herself behind, Carrie made her voice sound as dismissive as she could as she shrugged and told her, 'You may tell him whatever you choose. It is of no importance to me.'

'What? That you can even make such a comment shows you to be the unworthy, immoral creature that I always suspected you were,' the Countess told her imperiously. 'In your shoes—not that I would ever descend to such depths—I would hang my head in very shame and hide myself away from the world…' she announced theatrically.

'I wish,' Carrie muttered grimly, just under her breath, causing the Countess's face to burn scarlet with anger.

'You are a disgrace to our sex,' the older woman hissed. 'And totally unfit to—'

Both of them turned towards the door as it opened and Luc strode in.

'Carrie—Godmother…'

'Luc, there is something I must tell you,' the Countess announced, hurrying to him and giving Carrie a malevolent look. 'You can't marry this wretched creature!' she told him. 'I have always known her for what she was right from the start, when you… And now I have proof of it.' Turning away from Luc, she looked triumphantly at Carrie. 'No doubt you thought that what you had done was safely in the past, but the private investigation firm I hired were very thorough.'

Carrie knew what was coming, but she clung fiercely to her pride and refused to show any emotion.

The Countess was right about one thing. She *had* believed that what was in the past had already hurt her in all the ways it possibly could and that she had fought those demons—and won. Won the freedom to acknowledge her mistakes and lay them gently to rest. Won the right to peace of mind. Won the right to have her self-respect. And now here was the Countess, about to tear those rights from her…'

To her chagrin her self-control suddenly deserted her, and her voice was cracking with emotion as she was forced to beg, 'No. No…you must not.'

'You see?' the Countess told Luc exultantly. 'She knows what it is I have to reveal to you, Luc. She condemns herself out of her own mouth!'

'No…you mustn't,' Carrie repeated, but her voice was stronger now, and so was her purpose. Her glance met the Countess's with steely intent.

However, the Countess ignored her, announcing to Luc, 'This woman conceived another man's child and had it aborted. You cannot possibly marry her, Luc.'

A peculiar silence fell on the room. But instead of hanging her head in shame Carrie lifted it proudly and said quietly, 'That is not true.'

Inside she felt as though she was being torn apart—as though all her most private and sensitive feelings were being exposed—but she was not going to give either of her onlookers the satisfaction of seeing her pain.

'I have seen copies of all the medical documents,' the Countess revealed. 'They state quite plainly that you were pregnant and that the pregnancy was terminated! We all heard about the kind of life she led after she left here, Luc. Why, she even wrote to her father boasting about it. I remember how concerned he was. I don't suppose she even knows who the child's father was!'

'No,' Carrie repeated vehemently. 'It wasn't like that.'

'Then what *was* it like?' Luc asked her harshly.

It was the first time he had spoken, and Carrie turned to look at him, her eyes dark and haunted.

'Do you really want to know? Do you?' she challenged him wildly. 'Very well, then. I shall tell you. It was *your* child, Luc…yours!' She barely registered his indrawn breath or the look of shock in his eyes as she continued bitterly, lost in the pain of her own past. 'I did not have it aborted. At least…there were complications…it was an ectopic pregnancy… I didn't even know… I just… When the doctors diagnosed—when they told me—they said then that…that I had no option but to have the pregnancy terminated.'

Through the raw despair of the pain she had thought over and done with long, long ago, Carrie heard Luc saying curtly, 'Leave us, please, Godmother.'

'Luc, do not listen to her. She is lying…' the Countess was insisting, but Luc, ignoring her protests, was already walking her to the door, which he opened and then closed again behind her.

'Why was I never informed of any of this?' he demanded flatly as he came back to Carrie.

She couldn't bring herself to look at him—couldn't

bear to go any further into the past to the torment that lay there.

'*Why?* Why do you think? After the way you treated me,' Carrie began wildly, 'are you surprised that I didn't feel—?'

'You were carrying my child.' Luc stopped her curtly. 'Surely you must have realised that that changed everything?'

'I must have realised?' Carrie forced back a wild sob. 'Of course I realised. How could my life ever be the same? How could I ever be the same?'

She looked away from him, remembering how the doctor had urged her to get in touch with both her father and the father of her child.

'You will need their support,' she had been told.

'My father cannot give it and the baby's father will not,' she had replied.

In the end she had wept alone for the tiny life that might have been, and at the insistence of her tutor had gone, unwillingly at first but later gratefully, to see a counsellor at the university who had helped her come to terms with what had happened and to understand and accept the necessity of the medical steps that had been taken. Forgiving Luc had been hard, but forgiving herself had been far far harder.

'What I meant was that you must have realised that, had I been told you were carrying my child, then…'

'Then what? Then you would have married me?' Carrie challenged him wildly, shaking her head as she did so. 'Oh, I don't think so, Luc! You couldn't wait to be rid of me!'

Carrie took a deep breath. Here was her opportunity to tell him that he could no longer blackmail her, that Harry no longer needed his City job, and that if Luc needed a wife then he could find himself another one—because she was not going to marry him!

But before she could do so Luc burst out passionately, 'I should have been told! I should have been there. You should never have been allowed to go through such an ordeal alone.'

Carrie stared at him in disbelief. Was this Luc she was listening to? Luc who was pacing the floor, his voice raw with fury and anguish?

'Or *was* someone with you, Carrie?' he suddenly demanded savagely. 'Was another man comforting you, supporting you? Another lover who—?'

Carrie had had enough.

'Another man? Another lover? After what you'd done to me? Do you honestly think I would ever be stupid enough to allow myself to be hurt like that again? Since you I have never—'

Abruptly Carrie stopped speaking. In the thick silence of the room she and Luc looked at one another.

'Never?' Luc was frowning. *'Never?'* he repeated. 'If that is the truth, Carrie, then that's all the more reason why—'

'Highness— Oh, I am sorry…'

As the door burst open and a courtier came rushing in Carrie seized her opportunity and hurried out of the salon.

Why on earth had she made such a foolish and self-betraying admission? Just because she had been momentarily caught off guard by Luc's unexpected outburst of emotion, that was no reason for her to start behaving as though…

'Oh, miss—there you are… The hairstylist has arrived, and the make-up artist. They are waiting for you in your suite. Oh, and the housekeeper wishes to take you on an inspection tour of the royal bedchambers, to ensure that your room is to your liking.'

Automatically, Carrie started to hurry towards her suite.

Carrie lifted her head from her pillow and looked at her watch. It was just gone one o'clock in the morning.

It had been almost seven in the evening before she had finally been free of the last-minute wedding preparations. Luc, she had learned, had had some important meetings, so she had had dinner on her own.

Quite why she was here now, in bed in the castle instead of on her way home, she couldn't really explain.

Or could she? Sadly she touched her face, still damp from the tears she had cried in her sleep.

She had come to accept years ago that the child she and Luc had created between them was not meant to be, and the doctors had reassured her that there was no reason why she should not go on to have further healthy and normal pregnancies. She had even learned to tell herself, and believe that what had happened had been fate. After all, she could not have completed her education as a single mother, and—more importantly—she would never have wanted any child of hers to grow up with the kind of burdens that an illegitimate child of Luc's would have had, with a mother who had been rejected by its father. She had assured herself that one day she would meet a man with whom she would feel safe enough, loved enough, to create other children, and that when she did she would recognise just how facile and worthless the feelings she had had for Luc truly had been.

And she had believed what she had told herself. Until today. Until the door of her prison had swung open and she had realised that a part of her did not want to walk free—that, shamingly, a part of her still ached and yearned for Luc, that a part of her still stupidly believed in the ultimate fairy tale. The one that had the Prince falling in love with the peasant girl.

Pushing back the bedclothes, Carrie got out of bed and pulled on her robe. A full moon silvered the courtyard garden, and Carrie pushed open the doors onto her private balcony and went outside.

The Countess's cruelty had lanced a wound still un-expectedly filled with poison and not entirely healed.

Absently she walked down the narrow flight of stairs that led from her balcony into the garden below, and started to pace the gravel walkways, swept up in freshly painful memories.

She had fled S'Antander in acute distress, driven to England by her pride, but barely able to function on any-thing but the most basic level as she forced herself to act as though nothing had happened. As though she were not in the most acute emotional pain.

Unable to eat or sleep, she had focused as best she could on her studies, shutting herself totally away from any kind of emotional contact with other people, writing letters back to S'Antander to her father claiming untruth-fully that she was loving university life and that every night was a party and that every week brought a different admirer.

The reality could not have been more starkly different. She had virtually locked herself away in her room when she wasn't studying in the library.

She had known almost immediately that she was preg-nant, and had hugged the knowledge joyously to herself before the increasingly agonising abdominal pain she had been suffering had driven her to seek medical attention.

Sitting down at the side of the courtyard's fountain,

Carrie trailed her fingers in the water. Fat, lazy goldfish swam languorously past them.

Such a very few precious weeks—that was all she had had to imagine the dizzying joy of holding the child of the man she loved. Oh, how she had dreamed and planned. She could not have Luc but she would have his child… His son… She had so wanted her baby to be a boy. A boy who would look just like his father. A little Luc of her own. She would love him so… He would be the most precious thing in her life.

Her work had been forgotten as she'd daydreamed her way through the days, with hours at a time spent in rapt, awed and joyous anticipation. She had even begun to knit! Tiny little baby clothes! Practical plans, like how she would support herself or what she would tell her father, had had no place in her wonderful fantasy world.

But those plans and her happiness had all come crashing down the day the doctor had told her what he suspected.

How afraid she had been when she'd had to attend the hospital. She had gone there still a child, afraid for herself, afraid of losing the specialness that conceiving Luc's child had given her, but she had left as a woman, beyond fear, filled with aching grief and the pain of losing the life so precious to her on top of losing the man she loved.

There was a small splash as a tear rolled down her cheek and fell into the fountain, followed by another. Helplessly Carrie pressed her palms to her face and closed her eyes. She could not, *must* not break down here.

'Carrie?'

She froze as she heard Luc call her name, opening her eyes and jumping to her feet, desperate to escape. But Luc came after her, and moved far faster than she did, catching hold of her and pulling her into his arms.

'Carrie…Carrie… It's all right,' she heard him whisper rawly.

He was holding her, rocking her—comforting her, Carrie recognised weakly in disbelief, and she felt the emotions she had dammed for so long burst past her self-control, shaking her body with their intensity, filling her eyes with tears, racking her whole body with sobs that tore at her throat as she finally grieved for the life never meant to be in the arms of the man she had shared its beginning with.

'I had no idea,' she wept. 'I thought it was just something…a bad pain. I thought…I wanted our baby so much… I wanted to die when they told me that they were going to have to…'

'Oh, God, Carrie. Don't…please don't.'

She could feel Luc's arms tightening around her, could feel too the fierce, uneven thud of his heart beating against her, warming her, strengthening her. As suddenly as they had started her tears stopped, the brief violence of her grief leaving her finally fully released.

'There can be other children, Carrie. I know that does not take away the pain of what you suffered. I had to send you away…to let you go… You do not know how much I regret—'

'Allowing me to seduce you?' Carrie suggested dryly.

'So you acknowledge that *you* were the one to…?'

Carrie gave a small shrug.

'I was naïve. And besotted with you, Luc. I made it obvious how I felt.'

'You make it sound a very one-sided affair, Carrie, and it was by no means that. I have never denied and could never deny that I find you very, very desirable…'

His voice had dropped and he was looking at her in a way…

Carrie caught her breath as her heart lurched and her stomach hollowed. Wasn't there something she was going to say to him? she asked herself vaguely.

'You cannot imagine how jealous I was of all those lovers I now know you pretended to have.'

'You were?' Her voice sounded breathless, softly liquid…inviting.

'I was!' Luc agreed.

She could feel the warmth of his breath fanning her forehead…her nose…her lips…

'Luc!'

Was her soft murmur a protest or a plea? Had Luc even heard it? Or was he too busy tasting the warmth of her mouth?

'Do you remember the first time I made love to you?' Luc whispered.

'Yes,' Carrie whispered back.

'You trembled so in my arms—your whole body was quivering.'

'Because I wanted you so much…'

Just as she did now. Just as she was quivering now, Carrie recognised as he slowly rubbed his nose against her own and slid his hand beneath her robe to caress her body.

'In two days' time we shall be married…'

'Yes…' Carrie heard herself acknowledging meekly.

'And in nine months' time…'

Her whole body shuddered as he touched her intimately, and automatically she reached out for him, to him…

Silently Luc guided her back up the small staircase that led to her room, releasing her only to go and lock the bedroom door before returning to her side.

'I have been thinking about you all evening,' he whispered thickly to her as he cupped her face. 'In fact, if I am honest, I have been thinking about you ever since I looked out of my office window and saw you standing in the square.'

'I would never have come back to S'Antander to deliver Maria's message if I had known you would be here.' Carrie shivered as she spoke, her eyes darkening.

'It is fate,' Luc told her. 'Fate has brought us together again, and fate always has a purpose.'

'Please don't pretend that you have been longing for me all the time we have been apart, Luc.' Carrie warned him. 'You were going to marry Maria…'

'Were you longing for me?' he asked her.

Wryly Carrie looked at him.

'There were certainly times when I longed to be able to tell you how much I hated you!' she admitted hazily.

'So tell me, now.' Luc murmured as he caught hold of her and bent his head to kiss the small hollow at the base of her throat. His lips were playing expertly with her body, teasing small butterfly kisses against its vulnerability whilst his hands found her breasts, savouring their responsiveness to him.

Carrie expelled her breath in a light sigh, savouring the blissful sensation of Luc's touch. The slow stroke of his fingertips against her skin was awakening a need in her that was escalating past her control.

Gently, but oh, so determinedly, Luc took hold of her hand and guided it to his own body.

As she touched him Carrie felt him shudder openly with an intense male pleasure he made no attempt to hide.

'Do you remember the first time you kissed me there?' he asked her hoarsely, and continued without waiting for her reply. 'You were so shy, so unsure, and yet so eager to give me pleasure. You ran your lips over me and it felt delicate, aching, tormenting, making me hungry for so much more. And then you touched me with your tongue, stroking, seeking…'

Carrie heard him groan. Her heart was thudding in sledgehammer blows in response to the heavy erratic beat of his.

'It seems another lifetime ago,' she sighed.

'Another lifetime ago sometimes,' Luc agreed. 'But at others only yesterday.'

His hands left her body to cup her face and tilt it up to his own.

'Carrie! Carrie!' She heard him growl as her hand trembled against him and he lowered his head towards her, taking her mouth with slow, savage sweetness, the tip of his tongue thrusting past the barrier of her lips and opening up the sweetness they were protecting for his eager enjoyment.

Every touch, every kiss, was binding her even more relentlessly to him, Carrie recognised, but it was an imprisonment she gave herself up to willingly and wantonly.

When at last she lay naked on the bed, with Luc kneeling over her, she held him off for a few seconds, looking gravely into his face; his eyes were like her own, deep and dark with the strength of emotion.

'This was meant to be between us, Carrie,' he insisted softly. 'This…' He paused to kiss her slowly and tenderly. 'Us…' He kissed her again, this time deeply and intimately. 'You and me…'

Now she was the one reaching for him, holding her hand to his jaw as she covered his mouth with her own, tasting it with eager, aching longing.

She could see the passion burning in his gaze as she released his mouth, and he bent his head to caress the peak of one breast oh, so gently that she felt as though she was melting. And then more fiercely, very much more fiercely, so that she made a small keening noise of arousal, her hand reaching out to touch his hip and then the taut male curve of his buttock as she tried to urge him down towards her.

The way he was arched over her had an almost pagan primitiveness about it, an intimacy that caught at her heart and her senses.

'Carrie...' Her name was a soft moan of pleasure, exhaled on the thrust that carried him so powerfully and strongly into her body.

Eagerly Carrie received him and held him, drew from him the fierce culmination her own flesh desired.

He was still with her when she woke up an hour later, teasingly responsive to the touch of her hands but far less teasingly to the touch of her lips as she caressed him with more confidence than she had done that first time several years ago.

Now, instinctively she knew how to seek out his response, and she knew how to savour the sensation of his flesh, his arousal.

The sky was lightening when he finally released her from his arms and slipped from her bed with a last lingering kiss.

CHAPTER TEN

NERVOUSLY Carrie smoothed down the fabric of her wedding gown. She and Luc had not had any chance to be together alone since the night he had come to her in the garden, but by the end of today she would be his wife!

The previous day, during the rehearsal for the wedding ceremony, he had told her that the Countess had decided to make an extended visit to her cousin in Italy. He had squeezed her hand and given her a warmly tender look in the few precious, intimate seconds before they had been called upon to play their public roles.

They were to honeymoon on Jay's yacht, which he had put completely at their private disposal, and Carrie felt a sweet tremor of anticipatory pleasure shoot through her at the thought.

Now that their marriage was to be a 'proper' one, Carrie would have loved to be able to tell her family—in fact she was surprised that Harry hadn't heard of the wedding in the press. But then he and Maria would have been on their own honeymoon in Africa when the engagement was announced. Since it was too late for them to make it in time for the ceremony, she had decided instead to wait until she and Luc had returned.

What a shock Harry was going to get when he learned that she and Luc were married! And he and Maria weren't the only couple now planning excitedly for a future that would hopefully include children!

Luc could not have been more tender or caring about the child she—they—had lost.

'You should have informed me,' he had reproached her gently.

'How could I, Luc?' Carrie had reasoned. 'You had dismissed me—sent me away. I was eighteen. I felt rejected, worthless, broken-hearted.'

'I did what I believed I had to do,' Luc had returned sombrely. 'You were so young. I thought….was advised that your feelings were merely those of youthful infatuation, and that it would be kinder and indeed wiser for both our sakes for us to go our separate ways before we became any more involved with one another.'

'Advised? I suppose by that you mean that the Countess told you that?' Carrie had questioned quietly.

She had been able to see from his expression that his sense of loyalty was being strained by her question, and, respecting him for it, she had offered, 'Perhaps you weren't aware of it at the time, but even then your godmother was planning for you to marry Maria.'

Immediately Luc had shaken his head, reinforcing Carrie's growing belief that he had not known of the Countess's plans.

'Maria was a child of ten, then,' he had objected. 'The Regency was on the point of coming to an end and my godmother herself, as well as my advisers, stressed that my first and most important duty was to my country and my people, that I owed it to them and to my grandfather to concentrate on that duty. No, I think you must be mistaken there, Carrie,' he had insisted.

Carrie had not pursued the matter. Nor had she been able to bring herself to ask him why he had not explained both his position and his feelings to her himself, instead of allowing the Countess to do so for him, in such a deliberately cruel way.

Today, though, the unhappiness of the past was the last thing she wanted to think about.

The bedroom of her suite in the castle had two large windows—one with the balcony which overlooked the private courtyard garden, and another which overlooked the main public square outside the castle. This morning, from this window, she could see the finished effect of all the preparations which had been made to celebrate the Fifth Centenary and the wedding.

Extra floral displays had been added to those already put in place, and the bright early-morning sunshine sent shimmering prisms of colour dancing from the droplets of water dripping from the freshly watered flowers. The whole town had been decorated with wonderful displays in the colours of the Royal coat of arms—crimson, royal blue, gold and white—and from her window she could see the route of the short carriage drive she would be taking from the castle to the cathedral was a river of colour.

The tiny knot of excitement in her stomach, which had made it impossible for her to choke down anything more than a mouthful of the delicious breakfast she had been served earlier, sent out a shower of nervous bubbles of dizzy joy.

She could still barely take in what was happening—what had happened. But in the privacy of her bed at night she had rerun over and over again that precious interlude in the courtyard garden with Luc—admitting that, if anything, she was even more deeply in love with him now than she had been at eighteen. What she had felt for him then had been a girl's adoration; what she felt for him now was a woman's love.

Not even the thought of the relationship he had shared with Gina had the power to disturb her today, she acknowledged, as her bedroom door opened and Benita hurried in, carrying a small bouquet of cream roses and looking both excited and important. She handed them to Carrie and informed her that the hairdresser and the make-up artist were waiting for her, and that her attendants had all arrived and were being helped into their dresses by members of the design house's staff.

Carrie wasn't really listening to her. Instead she was touching the petals of one of the roses with a fingertip that trembled slightly, her lips curving into a tender smile as she read the message which had accompanied them.

I picked these myself this morning, from the courtyard garden. Luc.

That was all he had written—nothing more—but it was enough. In referring to the courtyard garden he was, Carrie knew, reminding her of the intimacy they had shared there, just as in telling her he had picked them himself he was telling her of his personal care for her.

Holding them up to her face, she breathed in their delicate perfume. Tonight, when she lay in his arms, she would tell him how much his gift had meant to her. Tonight...

Carrie tensed as the make-up artist flicked a final flourish of powder across her face, made sure that none of it was sprinkled on the wedding gown that Carrie was now wearing, and then stood back so that for the first time Carrie could see her reflection in the mirror.

A look of awed disbelief crossed Carrie's face as she stared at the familiar and yet unfamiliar image looking gravely back at her. Yes, that was her face, her nose, her eyes, her lips—but the woman in the mirror possessed an ethereal beauty that Carrie had never recognised in her own reflection before. This woman, dressed in heavy cream silk damask and wearing a heavy priceless tiara to secure the equally priceless antique Brussels lace of the veil which had originally been worn by Luc's grandmother, looked so breathtakingly, hauntingly fragile, with her huge eyes and slender body, that Carrie had to go up to the mirror and touch it to reassure herself that the delicate creature staring back was her.

Behind her, the room was crowded with her now silent attendants, standing in pairs. They comprised in the main daughters of Luc's courtiers, all of them wearing a plainer version of her own gown. Their gowns were sashed in the colours of the S'Antander coat of arms, and each girl carried flowers to match her sash.

Carrie's own flowers, a huge, trailing display of cream, white and green, were handed to her with careful reverence by the florist, whilst the hairdresser fussed and tweaked the already immaculate tendrils of hair which had been allowed to escape from her veil to add a modern and softening effect to the regal severity of her appearance.

When she moved her head the diamond earrings she had received from Luc this morning glittered even more fiercely than the diamonds in her tiara.

'Come…it is time…'

The stern voice of the dress designer broke the emotional silence gripping the room. Wordlessly Carrie turned towards the door.

She had never felt more nervous—or more alone. Just this morning she had spoken to her father and her stepmother, and to Harry and Maria, at Luc's instigation, to tell them that she was marrying Luc. Her father had been more pleased than surprised, and Harry had shocked her by telling her that he thought that she and Luc were very well suited.

'But I thought you hated him,' Carrie had protested.

'Not Luc,' Harry had assured her. 'Just the idea of him marrying Maria.'

Two uniformed footmen had appeared, and were now standing holding open the double doors where one of Luc's equerries, resplendent in a heavily gilt braided robe of office, waited to escort her to the state carriage in which she was to travel to the cathedral.

In keeping with tradition, as a bride she was to be kept enclosed within the carriage on her journey to the cathedral, so that no one could see her properly, but after the marriage she and Luc were to ride back to the castle in the open landau in which Luc was riding to the cathedral.

Frissons of nervous tension shook Carrie's body as she moved slowly to the door. The sheer weight of her gown combined with the tiara made moving any faster impossible.

The coach was pulled up outside the main entrance to the castle, and as she reached the castle doors Carrie heard a fanfare of trumpets. Then the doors were flung open with a flourish and she was blinking in the dazzling sunlight streaming in, her ears ringing with the wild cheers of the crowd waiting outside.

The size of the crowd and its exuberance took Carrie by surprise. It was true that Benita had warned her how excited everyone was about the double celebration, but Carrie had told herself that her maid was erring on the flattering side! Now she could see that she had not been.

The noise of the cheers greeting her must surely be intensified by the semi-enclosed square! As she walked as steadily as she could towards the waiting carriage, escorted by the equerry, the cheering seemed to increase in volume, and people began to throw flowers in the national colours into the square.

They rained down on the carriage and on the beautifully groomed pair of horses pulling it so that the road was a carpet of colour. With the window of the carriage wound down a little, to allow in some fresh air, Carrie could smell the scent released as the carriage wheels crushed the blooms.

Barriers had been erected all along the route, behind which the crowd stood ten deep, parents holding small children on their shoulders, their excited little faces catching Carrie's attention.

Suddenly the awesomeness and solemnity of the occasion hit her. She wasn't simply a woman marrying the man she loved; she was marrying a prince who had a deeply historic role to play, a deeply important commitment to keep! A commitment that was more important to him than the one he would make to her today in the cathedral? Carrie shook the thought away, struggling not to feel overwhelmed and daunted by the realisation of just how much her life was going to change.

When she was just supposed to be Luc's 'temporary bride', forced into an unwanted marriage with him, she had not given any thought at all to just what marriage to a man in his position would entail, what changes it would make to her own lifestyle. Why should she have done? There had been no need, as the marriage was to have been over within weeks of its beginning. And in the intensity of the intimacy which had only just developed between them she'd had neither the time nor the inclination to dwell on anything more than the fact that she and Luc were going to be together.

Now, though, she was actually aware of how much her life was going to change. When she left the cathedral today she would not be leaving it just as Luc's wife, but as the consort of a man who was dedicated to observing and protecting centuries-old traditions, a man whose people had expectations and needs which she, as his partner, would naturally be duty bound to play her part in helping him to meet.

Duty and responsibility. In many ways they were old-fashioned words in a modern world which lived by a modern code. But Luc was a man to whom they were very important—a man who took them extremely seriously.

Today, faced with the pomp and circumstance of what was happening, Carrie felt a sharp spike of panic, a fear of becoming a mere piece of window dressing in the life of the man she loved, but then, as the carriage pulled to a halt outside the magnificent fifteenth-century cathedral, a wonderful sense of calm and resoluteness filled her.

She would be her own person, as well as Luc's wife, a modern woman as well as the consort of a ruling prince; her training, her expertise in her profession could surely be put to a beneficial purpose—especially in a country such as S'Antander. She would insist to Luc that she was allowed a proper role to play within the state, she told herself sturdily as the carriage doors opened and the equerry handed her out; because from today she would be pledging herself not just to Luc but to his country, to its future and to its past.

Carrie paused before taking her first step into the cathedral. Its dark coolness was a blessed oasis of calm and peace after the noisy enthusiasm of the crowd outside.

The organist was playing a piece of music which had originally been written for the marriage of Luc's great-great-grandmother to his great-great-grandfather. She had been a Hapsburg princess!

As she entered the church Carrie could feel the rustle of excited curiosity. In the shadows the equerry stepped away from her, and another man, wearing not the brilliance of a uniform but the simple plainness of a dark suit, stepped towards her to take his place and escort her down the aisle.

As she turned to look at him Carrie's eyes widened. 'Dad…' she whispered in disbelief as her father came to her side and gave her arm a warm clasp.

'Luc arranged it. As soon as Luc contacted us on our Outback tour we knew we had to be here. We flew into Nice a couple of days ago. He wanted to keep it a surprise for you.'

Luc had brought her father here in secret, so that he could walk her down the aisle and give her away! The long, narrow path that led to where Luc was waiting for her shimmered as emotional tears filled her eyes.

'I always knew you two had a bit of a thing for one another, but I must say I never expected this,' she heard her father whispering to her with a big grin that told her how delighted he was as the distance between her and Luc narrowed.

Despite the fact that the rehearsal for the wedding had been meticulous, it had not, Carrie recognised, truly prepared her for the enormity of the occasion, nor for its length.

The tiara had begun to weigh heavily on her head, and Luc looked imposingly aristocratic and austere in the magnificence of his uniform. There was, Carrie felt shakily, something almost daunting and forbidding about him, and about the weight of tradition his shoulders carried so determinedly.

Her voice trembled when she said her vows, and so did

her hand when Luc slipped the wedding band onto her finger.

As an eighteen-year-old she had dreamed longingly of this occasion, fantasising about it and about Luc himself, but the reality far outweighed her youthful imaginings.

Luc's kiss was cool and brief, causing her to search his face with an anxious, intense gaze. In the courtyard garden he had been totally a man, rather than Prince and Ruler, but today, in this cathedral, he was very much what his destiny had ruled that he should be, and Carrie couldn't help but feel a little hurt by that.

'I now pronounce you man and wife,' announced the priest.

Triumphal music soared and filled the vastness of the cathedral as Luc walked Carrie back up the aisle. The ceremony had left her feeling drained and somehow vulnerable. She ached to be able to lean on Luc and feel his arms holding her, but this was not just a personal occasion and celebration; it was a public one. This morning, whilst she had been preparing for their wedding, Luc had already been in the cathedral, making a formal dedication to the state as its prince, and Carrie felt that the sombreness of that ceremony was somehow hanging over them, almost casting a shadow over them.

Telling herself that she was being over-emotional, she stood at Luc's side as the vast doors were drawn open and the crowd saw them standing together as man and wife for the first time.

The noise of cheering and exultation made Carrie's ears ache.

Luc had given an edict that no photographs were to be taken, since he did not want the occasion to be turned into a tabloid fest of dignity-shredding publicity.

His touch on her wrist was cool and light as she was helped into the landau by the waiting liveried footmen.

Seated opposite her, since there wasn't room for them to sit side by side, Luc immediately turned to acknowledge the cheers of the crowd. After a small self-conscious hesitation Carrie joined in and did the same. The crowd's cheers instantly increased in volume, people started to throw flowers, and by the time the landau had reached the castle it was filled with them. In the day's heat, the blooms were already wilting.

A small melancholic sadness touched Carrie's sensitive emotions. She glanced at Luc, suddenly needing the reassurance of a touch, a look that would tell her that beneath the uniform and the outer imposing appearance he was still the man she loved—the man who had held her and pleasured her—but was, it seemed, the whole of his concentration was on the cheering crowd.

Already Carrie was beginning to feel drained, and there was still the huge formal wedding breakfast to be got through!

As the landau pulled up in front of the castle Carrie leaned across and murmured to Luc, 'Thank you for getting my dad here. That meant so much to me.'

Instead of responding to her emotion, Luc was frowning. Almost curtly he told her, 'Naturally your father had to be here. For him not to be would have given rise to comment and speculation.'

Carrie looked uncertainly at him. Why was he suddenly being so formal and distant with her? She knew that this was a formal occasion, but surely in these few precious moments of privacy he could show her some tenderness? Surely he longed as much as she did for them to be together as man and wife…as lovers?

*   *   *

'Carrie!'

Standing waiting to receive their guests, Carrie stared in delighted disbelief at her brother and his wife.

As she was hugged and kissed, first by Harry and then Maria, Carrie stared at them both in bemusement.

'We flew in with Dad,' Harry told her happily. 'Luc arranged everything. We didn't say anything when you spoke to us on the phone as we wanted it to be a surprise.'

'I hoped that Luc would meet someone who would make him happy, but I never dreamed it would be you,' Maria chimed in, smiling as broadly as Harry. 'No wonder he was so willing to agree when I asked him to release some of my trust fund money so that Harry and I can buy the farm. And there I had been, dreading having to approach him but knowing that I had to as he is a trustee. He never said a word about you, though. We only heard about the wedding when he telephoned your father.'

The receiving line was anxious to move on, and Harry and Maria had moved away before Carrie could make any response. She looked towards Luc, who was speaking with a very elderly and very autocratic-looking man.

'A member of the Luxembourg ruling family,' her father whispered informatively to her, beginning to frown as he asked, 'Is it true that S'Antander is experiencing some political unrest, Carrie? I've overhead a few disturbing snippets of conversation whilst I've been here. I feel I've been hopelessly out of touch with things in Australia.' His frown deepened. 'I even heard someone discussing the possibility of Luc abdicating, but of course I know he would never do that. This country means everything to him. His grandfather made sure of that.'

'There have been problems,' Carrie admitted, and then stopped speaking as the receiving line advanced, making private conversation impossible.

Jay was the next in line, looking very American today, and far less physically like Luc than he normally did.

He gave Carrie a wink as he reached her.

'Real old-fashioned pomp and ceremony, this,' he whispered teasingly to her, before moving on.

At last it was over. Carrie ached to be free of her heavy gown and tiara. She and Luc had spent the last two hours circulating amongst their guests, but now it was time for them to retire to their separate suits to prepare for their honeymoon!

Benita was full of breathless excitement as she shooed Carrie's attendants out of the bedroom and helped Carrie to change.

'Your things have already been taken down to the harbour and put on board the yacht,' she informed Carrie happily. 'Oh, but you looked so beautiful. Everyone said so. You looked like a princess out of a story! Everyone will love S'Antander after today, and they will want to come here and spend their money here.'

Carrie felt too exhausted to reply. Her need to be free of the formality of the day—and its equally formal clothes—was almost a physical pain inside her. She ached for Luc and for the privacy to be with him as she wanted to be. Today, despite the fact that they had been married, he had seemed frighteningly distant from her—a withdrawn, austere stranger going through a necessary ritual.

As she shed the heavy weight of her wedding regalia Carrie also determinedly shed the unwanted weight of her sombre thoughts. Soon now she and Luc would be together as husband and wife. Today had been a public ceremony in which Luc had played a public role with which he was familiar but she was not. Tonight they would be meeting on an equal footing, as man and woman, as lovers! Her heart missed a beat and then started to race with anticipatory excitement and longing.

There were to be no formal 'going away' photographs either, in keeping with Luc's requested virtual press black-out, so Carrie was free to change into a pair of white silk evening pants and a soft halter-necked chiffon top, over which she was wearing a silk evening jacket which matched her pants. The outfit was very elegant and so-phisticated; it was also, Carrie admitted, very subtly sexy! The ties that fastened the halter-necked top were fastened in a bow at one side of her throat. Just thinking about Luc's lean fingers unfastening that bow made her heart flip and her body throb, suddenly throwing off its earlier physical tiredness.

There was a brief rap on the suite door and Carrie tensed holding her breath. Was it Luc?

Her spirits dropped a little when it turned out to be merely one of Luc's aides, who informed her politely that Luc wished her to know that for reasons of privacy and tradition they were to travel separately to the yacht, and that he would meet her on board.

Thanking him, Carrie told herself that it was silly of her to feel so emotionally disappointed and deprived just because she and Luc were not driving down to the marina together in the same car. They would be together soon enough now, after all—and not just for tonight, but for ever.

A discreetly dressed aide accompanied Carrie down to the marina.

The elegant cafés and restaurants along the waterfront were packed, the subtle nightscape lighting installed around the marina adding to the wealthy glow of an area that thronged with expensively designer clad women and their escorts.

That S'Antander was increasingly becoming an extremely cosmopolitan place was very evident, Carrie reflected. Everything about the town seemed lighter and somehow more open than it had done when she had spent her school holidays here. Then she could remember the marina area, with its yachts and their mysterious and forbidding owners, had been somewhere one was not encouraged to go. A sort of pall of secrecy and danger had hung over the area, which had been avoided by the majority of the local people. Now, though, according to Benita, the marina was a favoured local haunt of the state's élite, especially its younger members, and Carrie acknowledged as the car came to a standstill opposite Jay's yacht that S'Antander now had an enviable air of panache and stylishness.

No wonder it was being hailed as the tax haven to aspire to. But that status would be jeopardised by the current problems Luc was facing, Carrie admitted.

There was no Luc to welcome her on board the yacht, as she had secretly hoped.

Instead she was met by a member of the yacht's international crew. He escorted Carrie down to the huge owner's suite, where a steward was waiting to welcome her.

As he showed her round the suite's state-of-the-art facilities Carrie smiled attentively, but secretly all she wanted was for Luc to be here with her. The suite had its own private bathroom and dressing room, of course, in addition to an elegant sitting room with a private deck area, complete with its own Jacuzzi.

No expense had been spared in making the yacht a truly sumptuous hedonist's fantasy come to life, Carrie acknowledged after the steward had left her, having informed her that cocktails were to be served on deck, in one hour's time, followed by a special celebration gourmet dinner prepared for the newlyweds by the chef.

Impatiently Carrie paced the floor of the private sitting room. It was over an hour since she had come on board, and as yet there was no sign of Luc. The increasingly anxious enquiries she had made of the steward had not offered her any enlightenment as to his whereabouts. She tensed as she felt movement beneath her feet. Hurrying to the side of the cabin, she looked out to see the marina and the land disappearing as the yacht quickly picked up speed, headed for the open sea.

The yacht had put to sea!

Concerned, and beginning to panic, Carrie decided that she had had enough. Pulling open the cabin door, she hurried out of the suite, along the corridor and up onto the deck, intending to make her way to the bridge and demand that the Captain tell her what was happening and where Luc was.

She was halfway along the open deck, the speed of the yacht making her move cautiously in the high-heeled mules which matched her outfit but which personally she would never have chosen as deckwear, when she suddenly saw Luc ahead of her. He had obviously just emerged from the bridge and had his back to her. Relief flooded her and she hurried excitedly towards him.

'Luc!' she called out happily as she got within earshot of him.

The deck area where he was standing was only dimly lit, and for a second she felt merely confused when he made no move towards her, but simply stood stiffly watching her. But as she reached for him he turned his face away from her.

'Luc?' she protested, putting her hand on his jacket sleeve. 'Luc…'

CHAPTER ELEVEN

ONLY it wasn't Luc, she realised immediately. The flesh she could feel beneath her fingertips was quite definitely not Luc's! The arm she was touching was not Luc's and her body knew it!

The blood in her veins seemed to slow to a sluggish icy coldness and she shivered in panic and dread, her shocked brain trying to catch up with the speed of her body's instant realisation that the man beside her was not her husband.

He was turning to look at her now, and the slow chill of her blood became an instant freeze.

'Jay?' she protested, her eyes widening with disbelief.

A steward came up the gangway and announced formally, 'Chef wishes you to know that dinner will be served in half an hour, Your Serene Highness. Do you wish to have your pre-dinner drinks on deck or in the stateroom?'

His Serene Highness? Numbly Carrie waited for Jay to deny that he was any such thing, but to her shock he merely inclined his head and told the steward, in a passable imitation of Luc's cool tone, 'The stateroom will be fine, thank you. We shall be down in five minutes.'

Carrie would have said something immediately, but Jay reached out and gripped her arm firmly. His grasp was not painful, but the pressure conveyed his warning intent quite plainly.

Automatically Carrie responded to it, waiting until the steward had gone before bursting out, 'Jay—what is going on? Where is Luc? And why did the steward think *you* were Luc?'

When he made no response a horrible sense of foreboding overwhelmed her. Suddenly, out of nowhere, she could hear Luc's voice saying that he suspected someone was behind the activists, exploiting them for a purpose of his own. Carrie felt sick and faint with the intensity of her immediate suspicions.

Clenching her fist, she pulled away from Jay and demanded frantically, 'What have you done to Luc? Where is he? You'd better not have hurt him! You can't get away with this, Jay. You can't just…just dispose of Luc and take his place, no matter now many billions of dollars you have…'

Tears were flooding her voice, saturating it with distress as she went on fiercely, 'You could never take Luc's place. Never…'

As Jay looked at her and she saw the grim purposefulness in his eyes she was filled with fear—not for herself, but for Luc.

'We had better go for dinner, otherwise Chef will be mortally offended,' Jay announced coolly.

Carrie stared at him.

'Jay, I don't care how offended Chef might be,' she told him wildly. 'I demand to know what you have done with Luc and why you are impersonating him and I want to know now. Otherwise…'

The look he gave her was pure Jay, a rueful flash of immaculate American teeth that sliced his face with a wicked grin.

'Feisty lady,' he told her admiringly. 'That cousin of mine is one hell of a lucky guy. You really do love him, don't you?'

'What have you done with him, Jay?' Carrie repeated, ignoring his question.

To her dismay Jay burst out laughing and shook his head.

Taking hold of her arm, he told her, 'We'll talk about it over dinner.'

Carrie wanted to insist that they talk right here and now, but something in Jay's expression stopped her.

'Would you care to see the wine list, Your Highness?'

Carrie flashed Jay a murderous look as he took the proffered list with a coolly superior air that was more reminiscent of Luc at his haughtiest than Carrie wanted to acknowledge and quickly made his choice.

In any other circumstances the mere fact that the yacht had a wine cellar to choose from would have caused Carrie to marvel, but right now the luxuries afforded by Jay's expensive toy were of no interest to her whatsoever.

She ached to have the courage to denounce Jay, and had they been anywhere other than aboard his own personal yacht she knew that she would have done so.

Surely his captain and those who staffed the vessel for him must know he wasn't Luc?

As though he had read her mind, she heard Jay murmur dulcetly to her, 'Just in case you're wondering—and, being you, I'm sure that you are—all my regular crew are on a period of extended leave! Their substitutes know only that the yacht is owned by the billionaire cousin of His Serene Highness, and that it has been loaned to us for our ten-day honeymoon.'

Fear clawed and raked at Carrie's heart, made vulnerable by her love for Luc.

'You can't get away with this, Jay,' she protested. 'You can't just pretend to be Luc and...'

The way his eyebrows rose filled her stomach with ice.

What if it was already too late? What if he had...? Carrie licked her dry lips. No. No...she would have known...felt it if Luc was no longer alive; she was sure of that. She loved him so much it was impossible for him to have left this world without her somehow sensing it!

The steward had returned with their wine, and Carrie had to wait in a fever of frantic anxiety whilst the two men went through the ritual of pouring and tasting.

'I have taken the liberty of pre-ordering our dinner for this very special evening,' Jay was telling her in a faked, huskily intense voice.

The steward had moved away to the other side of the salon, and when he returned he was carrying a tray with two glasses of champagne on it.

Thanking him, Jay took one of the glasses and passed it to Carrie before taking his own.

'A toast!' he exclaimed theatrically. 'To my beautiful bride.'

As the steward moved discreetly away Carrie glared at Jay.

'I am not your bride,' she snapped. 'I have had enough of this...this farce, Jay. I want to know what is going on— and I want to know *now*,' she told him grimly.

'The steward will shortly be serving us our dinner,' he told her calmly. 'Until he has done so I have to warn you that for Luc's sake you must behave as though I am Luc!'

Warn her! Compressing her mouth, Carrie nonetheless did as Jay had told her. She was pretty certain now that whatever was going on Luc was not, as she had first thought, in any physical danger from his cousin. But what was going on? She wanted to know and she intended to know!

*　　*　　*

'More coffee, darling?'

Carrie feigned a sweet smile for the still hovering steward's benefit, under cover of which she glowered at Jay.

'No, thank you,' she gritted.

She could see Jay's grin as he told the steward, 'Thank you, that will be all. Please give Chef our thanks. The meal was truly superb—wasn't it, my sweet?'

'An unforgettable experience,' Carrie responded truthfully.

The meal had no doubt been the perfection of culinary art, but she had barely eaten. What she did know, though, was that her anger was certainly eating her!

'Right!' she announced, the second the door had closed behind the steward. 'What's going on? No more prevarication or delaying tactics. I realise how much you are enjoying this, Jay, but—'

'As a matter of fact, I am not enjoying it at all,' Jay told her soberly, suddenly looking very serious. 'Too much is at stake for that. This isn't a game, Carrie. And for Luc the stakes are so high, the risks so great…'

'For Luc?' Carrie questioned. 'What do you mean? Please explain.'

She had been as patient as she could be, but the small break in her voice betrayed the strain she was under much more than her previous explosions of anger.

Was it really pity she could see in Jay's eyes as his glance met hers?

'Very well. I warned Luc that this would happen, and I wanted him to tell you beforehand, but he felt there was too much of a danger, and that if he did you might inadvertently betray his plans. You know, of course, about the problems he has been facing with the activists? And I think you know why. They are objecting to the existence of secret accounts being held in S'Antander by certain persons whose politics and way of life are or have been in breach of certain basic human rights.'

Carrie frowned, nodding her head.

'The activists have sworn to take their protests as far as they have to in order to make those people remove their accounts from S'Antander—even if that means that the new, honest and legal tax exiles Luc has persuaded and encouraged to come here become so afraid and concerned that they leave and take their considerable money with them. The end, according to the activists, justifies the means, and they have said that they will stop at nothing either to force the account-holders under suspicion to leave or, if they won't, then force Luc to abdicate so that they may form a government which will make them illegal.'

Carrie digested what Jay was saying.

'But Luc himself could pass a law to make such accounts illegal if he wished. Surely…' she began, stopping when Jay shook his head.

'He could, technically, but these are powerful, dangerous people with long reaches and long memories. The last thing Luc wants is to turn the country into a bloodbath of attack and counter-attack. Because it wouldn't just be Luc himself who could become a potential target for their vengefulness,' he told Carrie sternly.

As Carrie's face paled Jay nodded his head sombrely.

'Luc cannot afford to offend these people—not just for his own sake, but for the safety and the lives of his people. He has tried to reason with the activists, to point out the dangers to them, but they are not prepared to listen to reason. Because of that, Luc decided that the only thing he could do was find a way to negotiate with the account-holders and somehow persuade them to voluntarily remove their accounts. However, he knew that if he were to do this publicly it would lead to more problems with the activists, who would claim Luc was pandering to the account-holders and secretly supported them. They might even suggest that he was in their power…their pay…'

'Luc would never—'

'Indeed he would not,' he agreed immediately. 'But I am afraid there have been rumours spread to the effect that Luc's grandfather had closer links with some of these people than was ever the truth. As we all know, mud sticks, and whilst Luc believes that many of the activists are genuine in their beliefs and aims there is a core within them that is secretly dedicated to bringing about the downfall of Luc as S'Antander's ruling prince. That core is not really so concerned about the moral aspect of these secret accounts; it is just using them to cover its own plans to have Luc deposed and to take over the country—perhaps not publicly, but rather to control it from the shadows. S'Antander is in a unique position in many ways, and offers many opportunities and benefits to people wanting to use it for their own gains!'

'I understand what you are saying,' Carrie agreed. 'But I don't understand why any of this should necessitate you masquerading as Luc!'

'Well, I must admit I was dubious myself at first, when Luc approached me—but, being Luc, he managed to talk me round. He needed time and privacy to meet with these secret account-holders and diplomatically persuade them to move their accounts elsewhere without offending them. As Luc pointed out to me, he cannot afford the luxury of allowing his personal feelings to control his actions. He has to put his country first; that is his solemn duty and responsibility—a duty and responsibility he swore to uphold the day he was crowned as S'Antander's ruler,' Jay told her sombrely.

'Luc felt that his marriage and subsequent honeymoon would act as the perfect cover for him to slip out of the country unnoticed and engage in the necessary negotiations and discussions. Obviously someone had to be seen to go on honeymoon, someone posing as Luc, which was where I became embroiled in his plans. Originally, of course, he was planning to marry Maria,' Jay told her carelessly, giving a small shrug whilst a tiny icy-cold and painfully sharp lump formed deep inside Carrie's stomach. 'But then Maria threw a real spanner in the works by eloping with your brother, and Luc had no option…'

But to marry me,' Carrie finished quietly for him.

Jay looked uncomfortable.

'Well, of course it was different with you… You and Luc have a shared past, a shared relationship—feelings which seeing one another again rekindled. I am sure it must have complicated the situation for Luc, but he was determined to go through with his original plans.'

'I am sure that he was,' Carrie agreed coldly. The frozen knot in her stomach was growing larger by the heartbeat, and very soon now it would be filling her middle and reaching out into her veins, into the blood they carried to her heart, chilling that too, freezing it…freezing to death her love, destroying it as Luc had destroyed her! Not once now, but twice. Why, oh, why had she allowed this to happen? Why had she not realised…?

No wonder he had been so keen to make love with her! By that stage he must have already known that he could no longer hold the threat of harming Harry over her—thanks to Maria's request to him to release her trust fund—and, being Luc, he would have immediately taken steps to replace that hold with another even more powerful one. A hold that would bind her willingly to him instead of unwillingly! How diabolically clever he had been…and how unbearably cruel! He had even cynically and cold-bloodedly used the death of their child to make her vulnerable to him…

And to think she had been stupid enough to believe that he cared about her! He didn't care at all! In fact he cared as little for her now as he had done all those years ago, when he had instructed his godmother to send her away from him! He was using her now as he'd used her then. And no doubt he wouldn't hesitate to cast her aside once again when his problems were resolved.

The lump of ice was replaced with a white-hot burning pain, a savage anger that twisted and maimed all the love and softness inside her, turning it into bitterness and hatred. She was wiser now, though, than she had been at eighteen, and there was no way she was going to allow Jay to see how she felt. No way she was going to allow anyone to guess how she felt until she'd had the opportunity to unleash those feelings on Luc himself!

'My, the two of you have been busy,' she forced herself to say thinly.

The look Jay gave her warned her that her act was not totally convincing.

'You're shocked, I know. It was a very hard decision for Luc not to tell you.'

For a moment Carrie's anger was so choking that she couldn't even speak, but somehow she managed to swallow back her fury and agree with Jay—at least outwardly.

'Yes. It must have been.'

'He wanted to protect you,' Jay told her.

He wanted to *use* me, Carrie thought bitterly—but of course she wasn't going to voice her thoughts.

'Using my yacht for your honeymoon was a brilliant idea, don't you think?' Jay asked enthusiastically. 'I have to hand it to Luc for coming up with that, although I've got to admit it felt rather odd, being driven from the castle to the marina wearing Luc's uniform. And then, of course, I had to keep myself out of your sight until after we had sailed. Oh, and by the way, I have to warn you I shall be sleeping in the adjoining cabin to yours. There are interconnecting doors, but naturally they will remain closed throughout the voyage.'

'Indeed they will!' Carrie agreed woodenly.

'I just hope that ten days is long enough for Luc to complete his negotiations. He has already set things in motion, of course…'

'Of course,' Carrie echoed, before saying with exquisite politeness, 'It's been a long day—would you mind if I went to bed?'

At any other time Jay's look of relief would have amused her.

'You really are being good about all of this, Carrie,' he praised her warmly. 'I must admit I was a bit apprehensive about how you'd react when you realised I wasn't Luc.'

'But Luc, I take it, had no such apprehensions?' Carrie couldn't resist asking.

From the look in Jay's eyes there had obviously been more of an acid bite to her words than she had intended.

'He had no other option,' Jay told her loyally. 'For your own protection it was safer that you didn't know…'

'Indeed! I must say I felt very "protected" when I believed that he was in danger,' Carrie told him coolly.

'You obviously love him one hell of a lot,' Jay said roughly.

Carrie turned her head away before she replied, so that her quiet, 'Yes, I did,' didn't reach Jay's ears.

Carrie looked at her watch. In another few hours they would be docking, the 'honeymoon' over.

Jay had done his best to keep her entertained and amused over the last ten days. Since officially they were on honeymoon they had not had any royal duties to undertake, and Jay had carefully made sure that they stayed out at sea, rather than putting in to any European ports. There had been plenty for her to do on the yacht, though; it had its own mini-gym, and was well stocked with the latest books and DVDs. Jay had even attempted to teach her to deep-sea fish. But despite Jay's best efforts it was Luc and what he had done to her, the way he had so callously used her, that had occupied most of Carrie's thoughts.

If she had been a different type of woman she could have sustained herself by plotting her revenge—and what a revenge she could have had! Oh, yes, she had had plenty of time to dwell on what Luc had done to her! How much he had hurt her! All those long, empty hours at night when she had lain awake in the huge bed she had expected to be sharing with him. She had tried to use those nights productively, to destroy her love for Luc as she knew she ought to be doing. If only she had been different from the way she was… But she struggled to turn off her emotions like a tap.

Miserably Carrie wondered when she would stop crying. Crying as though something deep inside her heart was making it bleed!

Sombrely Luc contemplated the scene outside the window of his small, nondescript rented room. He had booked it in a fictitious name and had used it hardly at all. Tonight, if all went as he hoped it would go, he wouldn't be using it at all—because he would be on his way back to S'Antander, with the written agreement of certain parties to the removal of their assets from S'Antander's bank vaults.

His grandfather had done what he had thought best for his people by allowing these accounts to be opened in the first place, and Luc had to do the same by having them removed. For his grandfather the enemy had been poverty and ignorance, and, while Luc acknowledged that his grandfather had been wrong not to ask many questions of those who had opened bank accounts in S'Antander, he knew that to help the poor and uneducated his grandfather had sold his conscience. And now their descendants reviled the man responsible for their prosperity and comfort.

Luc could not entirely blame them, just as he could not entirely blame his grandfather. Times and conditions had changed. And now, just as his grandfather had done, he too was having to make choices and decisions which would protect the state and the people he was morally responsible for.

There had been many times over the last ten days when he had feared that all his efforts might fail. He'd received angry looks and words from the men he was negotiating with which had warned him against trying to move too quickly or showing any sign of what he truly felt.

In the end his most powerful weapon had been the threat of danger and exposure.

'I urge you for your own sakes to take this opportunity to remove your assets now, quietly and discreetly,' he had told them. 'I cannot guarantee your safety if your identities should become known. The insurgents in S'Antander—'

'They can be annihilated,' one of the men had said coldly, and Luc's stomach had dropped, his flesh crawling at the look in the man's eyes, but he had refused to drop his own gaze from the menacing basilisk stare.

As arranged, he had had no contact with Jay—just in case any suspicions might be aroused—but that did not mean that the occupants of the yacht had been forgotten. Especially not one of them!

Carrie! He had thought he had everything planned, every detail refined, everything under control—until the day he had looked out of his office window and seen her standing there in the square, and he had...

He tensed as his mobile rang. Flicking it open, he answered the call.

The speaker on the other end of the line merely announced tersely, 'They've agreed,' but it was enough!

Luc gave the room a last brief look. He would not be sleeping here tonight. Thank goodness! And thank goodness, too, things now looked likely to work out as he had hoped!

CHAPTER TWELVE

IT WAS disorientating to have an unmoving floor beneath her feet again, Carrie acknowledged as she stood in the middle of the enormous bedroom she had been escorted to on her return to the castle. This was to be her new bedroom: the marital bedroom. Automatically her gaze was drawn to the communicating double doors which linked her room to Luc's.

Luc! Grimly Carrie walked across the thick-pile carpet and stood in front of the window. Like that of her previous room it looked down into the private courtyard garden, but, unlike that one, it shared its large balcony with the room belonging to Luc.

Carrie picked up the glass of iced tea she had ordered and sipped it. She had arrived back at the castle less than an hour ago, having been driven there under cover of darkness. She presumed that Luc was already in the castle, since she could hardly be expected to return from her 'honeymoon' on her own, but as yet she had not seen him.

But when she did!

She tensed and swung round as she heard a discreet rap on the outer door of her room, but when Benita emerged from the dressing room, where she had been unpacking Carrie's things, to answer the door, it was only a footman who was standing there.

'His Serene Highness wishes to apologise to the Princess for the fact that he is at present involved in a meeting, but he will join her for dinner in one hour's time

161

and they will be dining *en cabinet*,' the footman announced formally to Benita.

A thin, bitter little smile stretched Carrie's mouth as she listened. How very thoughtful of Luc to send her his apologies! And how very hypocritical!

It was only the depth of her pain and her desire to tell him exactly what she thought of him that was fuelling her now. It overcame the temptation to refuse to go down for dinner, and told her instead that the sooner she informed Luc that their marriage was over and that she felt nothing but contempt for her new husband the better.

Something—maybe a sense of pride, of outrage, and of pure, burning female fury—compelled her to dress for the dinner with all the concentration and attention to detail of a general preparing his troops for war!

To Benita's obvious delight she eschewed the sensibly practical underwear she had brought to S'Antander with her and chose instead to wear a set of the deliberately sensual and provocative matching scraps of silk and lace masquerading as underwear that had arrived at the castle as part of her trousseau.

The bra, halter-necked and low-backed, was nothing more than a whisper of cream silk and exquisite delicate lace butterflies that stroked tenderly against the warm tan of her skin, whilst the briefs were cut low on the hips, where they fastened with one tiny button, and were styled as very, very brief boxer shorts, with matching lace butterflies edging their legs. Her legs, sleek and tanned from the hours she had spent in the sun in the privacy of her own sunbathing area, did not need any kind of cover, and the beauty therapist on board the yacht had only this morning given her a pedicure—her toenails gleamed with shimmering polish.

Was it out of a desire to punish Luc or a desire to

punish herself that she had decided to wear the same outfit she had chosen for their first night on board the yacht? Did it matter just so long as in wearing it she remembered the pain of that evening and its revelations?

Her skin, like her nails, gleamed sensuously beneath the glowing light cast from the wall sconces along the corridor as the footman escorted Carrie to the dining room which was not, as she had expected, the large, formal dining room she was already familiar with but a much smaller and more intimate one.

A sharp burn of anxiety scoured her senses as the footman bowed and retreated, leaving her alone.

The room was lit only with vanilla-scented candles. Its walls were covered in rich red damask to match the tall dining chairs, and decorated with ornate gold-framed mirrors.

Within seconds of the footman leaving the pair of double doors on the opposite side of the room were thrown open and Luc strode in.

And it *was* Luc. Carrie could sense that it was him, feel that it was him with every pore in her body and with every savage, hurting ache of her heart.

Silently she observed him. Was his face a little thinner? Were the high cheekbones a little more pronounced?

Carrie watched him as he came towards her, her body stiffening as he reached her and took hold of her hands, his head dipping. Resolutely she neither flinched nor moved until the very last minute, so that the kiss intended for her lips merely grazed against her cheek.

She could see the hot smoulder in his eyes as they narrowed questioningly. Did he really need to question her reaction? His arrogance was unbelievable! Didn't he realise how lucky he was that her pride and her self-control prevented her from turning into the hellcat her pain demanded and clawing that smooth male flesh until it bled as she was bleeding inside?

'I'm sorry I wasn't here to greet you when you got back,' she heard him telling her smokily. 'I had planned to be, but unfortunately a necessary meeting ran late. I thought tonight that it would be more…intimate if we dined here,' he continued, releasing her to go over to the wine cooler standing to one side of the round table.

Unrelentingly Carrie watched as he removed a bottle of vintage champagne and deftly opened it, filling two crystal flutes and then picking them both up and coming back to her.

Handing her one, he told her, 'To us, Carrie, and to—'

He broke off as a discreet knock on the door heralded the arrival of their dinner.

Any kind of personal or intimate conversation was impossible whilst they were dining, with two footmen hovering over them and various courses of food being carried to and from the table. But she wasn't in any hurry. She could wait and anticipate the pleasure of telling Luc just what she thought of him.

She wasn't particularly hungry either—scarcely able to eat more than a mouthful of each course.

'Is something wrong?' Luc asked her frowningly, when her plates continued to be removed with the food barely touched.

'Wrong?' Carrie looked at him in disbelief. 'Do you really need to ask me that?' she demanded as the anger fizzed inside her like the bubbles in the champagne she had drunk earlier. 'You—'

She fought back the savage indictment she was longing to make as the footmen reappeared. She took a cooling gulp of her wine to calm herself down, and then another as she felt the soothing spread of the mellow liquid spilling through her body.

At last the meal was over, and Luc dismissed the footmen.

'Coffee?' he asked, indicating the full coffee pot that had been left.

Carrie shook her head, not trusting herself to speak. How dared he do this to her? How dared he put on this cynical show of post-honeymoon intimacy when in reality...

She saw the candle flames flicker as Luc moved, walking not towards her but towards the doors he had come through earlier.

'Come here,' he commanded her softly.

Grimly Carrie went to him.

'Luc—' she began fiercely, but he didn't allow her to get any further, wrapping one arm around her and lowering his head so that he could whisper in her ear.

'Have I told you yet how beautiful you look tonight, Carrie?'

He was kissing the side of her neck with open hunger and Carrie felt herself begin to shudder.

Luc was pushing open the doors behind him with his free hand, and as they opened Carrie could see through them into the bedroom that lay beyond them.

'You don't know how often these last ten days I've dreamed about doing this,' Luc groaned as his hand cupped her face and his mouth found hers, taking it in a kiss of fiercely intimate male passion.

Fury exploded inside Carrie as she stood still and unmoving in Luc's embrace. She could feel his realisation of her lack of response when his hold on her slackened and he released her mouth.

'What is it?' he asked, frowning at her.

'What is it?' Carrie glared at him. 'Do you really need to ask me that, Luc? Did you really think I wouldn't realise the truth?'

She watched as he closed his eyes and then opened them again.

'Carrie, I couldn't tell you. I know that Jay has explained everything to you. You must understand—'

'*Must?*' Carrie checked him with chilling contempt. 'No, Luc, you are the one who must understand—that I will not be used in the way you have tried to use me.'

'Carrie, I had no choice.' Luc's voice was stern now. 'My duty to my country—'

'Comes before everything else. Yes, I know that, thank you, Luc, Well, for your information, so far as I am concerned my first and foremost duty is to protect *myself*!'

'Carrie, I promise that you weren't in any danger. I would never expose you to danger.' His voice had softened, and suddenly he groaned. 'Oh, Carrie! Carrie! Why are we fighting when all I want to do is take you in my arms and...? When all I want to do is this...' Luc finished thickly, and, taking her off guard, he picked her up bodily in his arms and, kicking the door closed behind him, carried her over to the huge bed.

Lying on her back, with Luc's weight pinning her down, it was impossible for Carrie to move, and impossible for her to speak as Luc took possession of her mouth, kissing her with a fierce, deep hunger whilst his fingers tugged impatiently at the bow securing her halter-neck top—just as she had fantasised about him doing when she'd put it on the first night of their honeymoon.

Her anger seared her, but treacherously her body was already aching with white-hot anticipatory pleasure, responding to Luc's hungry passion as though it was entirely independent of her brain and her emotions.

Whilst her head screamed with silent anger her body moaned with equally silent enjoyment. She could see the dark splay of Luc's hand against her flesh, feel its heat and feel her own response.

Luc's lips scorched the flesh exposed by the delicate lace of her bra, his hand pushing the fabric away, his whole body stilling as he revealed the smooth, tanned globe of her breast.

She could feel him looking at her

'You've been sunbathing without a top!' It was a statement, not a question, and his voice was curt and foreboding. 'With Jay?'

Carrie stared at him. He actually sounded as though he was jealous!

'I've been on a cruise, Luc,' she reminded him sharply. 'A honeymoon cruise…supposedly with my husband.'

'I am your husband,' he told her tersely.

'No,' Carrie responded coldly. 'You are the man who married me, Luc. You're not my husband and you never will be.'

She could see the anger and disbelief darkening his eyes.

'What on earth are you talking about?'

'I am talking about the fact that you have deliberately and cold-bloodedly used me, Luc. Did you really think I wouldn't have the intelligence to put two and two together and come up with four? I'm an economist, remember— facts and figures are my business. It must have really upset your plans when you discovered that you weren't going to be able to blackmail me into marrying you any longer by threatening to harm Harry!'

She was still lying on the bed underneath him, but she could feel the coolness of air between them as he lifted his head to stare down into her face.

'Don't try to deny it, Luc,' she warned him. 'Harry told me about Maria needing your permission to withdraw money from her trust fund to buy a farm. Obviously you knew then that it wouldn't be long before I learned that Harry no longer needed his City job. But then fate stepped in on your side, didn't it? And your godmother handed you the very thing you needed, didn't she? What a relief that must have been for you, Luc! All you had to do to make sure I went through with the marriage that had become such an essential part of your plans was to offer me a little bit of fake sympathy and understanding, to pretend to feel regret and remorse. And how convenient that you happened to be there when I was at my most vulnerable. Little did I know, when I was crying in your arms for the past, and what might have been, that you were deliberately using that vulnerability for your own ends!'

Carrie's mouth twisted. 'Blackmail and sex. Two of the most powerful weapons there are. And you have used them both unflinchingly, haven't you, Luc? But then of course you had to, didn't you? You have your duty to your country, after all, and that is far more important than anything or anyone else! Well, not to me it isn't, Luc. And—'

'This is crazy.' Luc stopped her savagely. 'I have no idea why you are feeding your imagination with such implausible scenarios, Carrie. Do you realise how…how offensive and insulting your accusations are? How hurtful?'

'Hurtful?' Carrie gave him a contemptuous look. 'Well, they say that the truth hurts, don't they, Luc? Did you get what you wanted, by the way? Were your negotiations successful?'

She could see him frowning as he told her tersely, 'As a matter of fact, yes, they were.'

'Good. Then that's all that matters, isn't it? At least it is to you.'

'Carrie, will you stop this?' Luc demanded harshly. 'I can understand that you might feel upset that I didn't explain to you what I was doing, but that was for your own sake and because—'

'No, it wasn't, Luc. Nothing you have done has been for *my sake*. You have used me, cynically and…unforgivably. What kind of man are you, Luc? You even took me to bed, treated me as though I was the most desirable woman you had ever met to make sure I wouldn't leave. What a noble sacrifice, Luc! What a pity you can't make it public. I'm sure that your country would be impressed to know what you forced yourself to do in the name of duty. How *did* you manage to do it, by the way? Pretend to yourself that I was your mistress? Well—'

Carrie gave a shocked gasp as Luc gripped her shoulders and told her savagely, 'That's enough. For your information no *pretence*, as you call it, was necessary. I'm a man, Carrie, and you are—'

She could see the anger flash through his eyes, and a kick of responsive emotion burst through her own body.

'A man who makes love or rather has sex out of duty!' she goaded him. 'Oh, yes, I know that.'

'Do you? Well, then, this won't come as any surprise to you, will it? After all, as you reminded me earlier, we are married. But I am not yet your husband, Carrie in every sense of the word. An omission which I intend to remedy right now…'

'No,' Carrie refused, suddenly realising her danger. But it was too late.

Luc's muttered 'Yes!' was burned against her lips,

smothered by the pressure of his tongue-tip forcing apart her lips.

Carrie had thought that all the vulnerability had been drawn out of her by her own pain, but now she realised that she had been wrong. Something fierce and elemental deep within her own flesh leapt into life at Luc's touch, meeting and matching the savagery of his passion, feeding and sharing it.

The insistence of his mouth, the touch of his hands, the hunger and the anger she could feel within him—Carrie met and matched them all. Here, now, in her arms, Luc was a man and not a prince; like her he was driven by the dark intensity of need; like her he could not control what he was feeling. They were meeting, Carrie recognised fiercely, as equals—and as adversaries.

When she left him, when he was without her, if she wanted anything she wanted him to know what he had lost—what he could have had if he had not deliberately destroyed it. Her love would have been a priceless gift, and he had spurned it. But he could not reject her body, nor his own desire for it. Luc was as helplessly enmeshed in the hunger tormenting him as she was in the aching need he had seeded inside her.

Carrie instinctively knew that each touch, each kiss, would be written into her senses for ever. Her body would never, ever feel like this again, want like this again, or love like this again.

She cried out as Luc entered her and she heard his guttural moan of pleasure as her body closed wantonly around him.

Each thrust of his flesh within her own rocked her senses, taking her deeper and deeper into a world where only the two of them existed, where all that mattered was the final culmination of their shared driving urge. Reality, pride and the future fell away. There was just the here and now. Luc kissed her, a fierce, passionate possession of her mouth that took her breath and with it her sharp cries of pleasure as her body shook with the intensity of her orgasm. The fierce contractions were only just dying when she felt Luc's own release.

Wrapped tightly in one another's arms, they felt their heartbeats gradually separate from their shared rhythm and return to their own.

Carrie felt Luc's hand against her skin, cupping her jaw, turning her face towards him. Relieved of the sharp ache of her own physical need, she fought to control the danger of this special time of sweet sadness, when a woman's emotions were notoriously at their most vulnerable.

Luc bent his head to her. She could feel the cooling dampness of the sweat on his skin. His lips brushed hers slowly. A mist of tears she couldn't quite stop hazed her eyes at his gesture of what could be described as tenderness. Faked tenderness, she reminded herself sharply as she made her lips remain cool and unmoving beneath his.

She could feel him looking at her, and when she turned her head towards him she almost winced beneath the probing intensity of his questioning gaze.

'Using me as a substitute for your mistress doesn't change a thing, Luc,' she told him cuttingly, curling her lip at him. 'First thing tomorrow morning I shall be leaving S'Antander, and this time I won't ever be coming back!'

Without another word she pushed herself away from him and reached for her discarded clothes.

'Carrie.' She could hear the ominous note in his voice but she ignored it, calmly redressing.

A vast protective numbness had thankfully engulfed her so that her movements were steady and mechanical, almost as though they were being actioned by some means of remote control.

'For a start, I do not have, nor ever have had a mistress, and if—as I think you must be—you are referring to Gina, then for your information she and I were never lovers!'

His disclosure must have shocked her, Carrie realised distantly, but she refused to respond to Luc's comment. What was the point? Nothing could change the way he had used her, and nothing could change the fact that he would do so again and again if he ever felt the need, in order to do his duty and protect S'Antander. Other people might find that aspect of his personality praiseworthy, and indeed were she one of his subjects she might too, but she was not. She was the woman who loved him, who wanted and needed to know that their love was shared, that their relationship was special, sacrosanct, and, however emotional it might seem, she needed to know that she held first place in his heart just as he did—or rather, had done, she amended quickly—in hers!

CHAPTER THIRTEEN

IT WAS a new day, the sun was shining, the sky was blue, and the castle and its environs looked picturebook-perfect. But none of those things had the power to touch her this morning, Carrie acknowledged as she walked out of the castle and into the square for nearly the last time.

Her cases were packed—minus the designer clothes that Luc had bought her. There was nothing she wanted to take with her from these last few weeks other than the necessary protection from the pain Luc had caused her to guard her through the aching loneliness of the time that lay ahead. By reminding herself of that pain she would be able to ignore any weak, impulsive longing for him and learn to overcome it!

The square was busy with visitors come to exclaim over the castle and its history, and the outdoor tables of the small cafés facing onto it were filled with customers. A group of young men seated at one of the tables briefly caught Carrie's attention, more because of their silence than anything else.

She was almost halfway across the square when she heard Luc call her name. Her body stiffened, and for a second she was tempted to ignore him, but somehow she discovered that she was turning round to face him, watching as he stood looking at her from his vantage point on the steps leading up to the main entrance of the castle.

As he started to walk down them a small tremor ran through her. Against her will she was remembering the previous night and the intensity of the passion they had shared. For some people such a passion would more than compensate for whatever else might be lacking in a relationship. Indeed, some people would no doubt consider that she was a fool to turn her back on it. Some people...

'Carrie!' Luc called her name again.

She blinked as she heard the warning in Luc's voice, bemused when she saw him running towards her. In the distance she could hear noises, shouts, protests, screams of fear and shock, and then all the breath was knocked out of her lungs as Luc reached her, knocking her to the floor, where the impact of his body falling on top of her own drove the breath from her and obliterated the brilliance of the sunshine.

All around her she could hear sounds—the sounds of panic. She was aware of screams, people crying, sirens and the rush of feet. She could see feet running towards them, uniformed legs ending in polished boots. Someone was pulling Luc from on top of her, and as they did so she could see the bright red drops of blood splashed on the cream stone.

She could hear someone crying over and over again—'No—no...no. Please God, no...' And then she realised that the agonised voice she could hear was her own. Hands were reaching down to help her up, faces were looking into her own with expressions of anxiety, shock and concern.

'Luc...Luc...Luc...'

She was still sobbing his name as they put her in the ambulance, and just before it drove off she saw the guards marching away the group of young men she had seen earlier.

On the ground where they had lain only moments before was a gun, which one of the guards carefully covered with a cloth before removing it.

*   *   *

Carrie paused and took a deep breath, looking up at the blue summer sky.

It was almost six weeks since the appalling incident outside the castle in which Luc had been shot, taking the bullet which had been meant for her.

'Ready?'

She looked up as she felt Jay's light but protective touch on her arm and fiercely tried to banish the shadows from her eyes. Banishing them was at least something she could attempt to do—unlike those darker shadows that surrounded her spirit and her innermost self.

The black car with its heavily tinted windows was already drawing up alongside the private entrance to the castle.

Following the shooting she had had to delay her plans to leave S'Antander. For one thing, she had been told that medically she was in too much shock, and then later her position as the Prince's wife had made it impossible for her to do so. Soon, though, the duty she had had to assume would be at an end and she would be free to leave.

Only she knew how much she was dreading the ordeal that now lay ahead of her, and she prayed it would be her final one.

A grim-faced uniformed chauffeur got out of the car.

Carrie's mouth had gone dry, and her heart was pumping enough adrenalin around her veins to fuel a moon-bound missile. She couldn't bring herself to look at the waiting black car. Thankfully Jay had stepped past her and was walking towards it.

The chauffeur was opening the door.

Carrie ached to look away but she couldn't bear to. Holding her breath, she watched as the tall familiar figure uncoiled itself from the passenger seat and stepped out, lifting his face towards the sun and taking a deep breath before walking calmly towards her.

Carrie felt as though the rapid thud of her heart was going to choke her. Even though she knew they were not open to public view in the square, her mind kept on running over what had happened there. She wanted to rush to Luc and drag him inside to safety, to beg him to hurry, and all the time her gaze was frantically searching the protected empty space surrounding the car and the castle entrance, which she knew was heavily guarded, just in case there was any danger there.

The last six weeks had taken a terrible toll on her. Guilt, pain and fear—she had known them all.

When she had followed Luc to the hospital after the shooting she had been told that he had been very lucky and simply suffered a gunshot wound to his shoulder. But later complications had developed; the wound had become infected and Luc had gone into a coma as the poison spread through his system.

For almost a week everyone had feared that he would die.

Carrie had sat with him night and day through the long hours of his fight for life, willing him to recover, reminding him over and over again of how much his country, his people needed him.

She would, she knew, never know if any of her words had reached him, just as she would never know if he had heard her final exhausted admission that she loved him.

At first she had refused to allow herself to believe it when she had been told that he was starting to recover, but then he had regained consciousness, and after that Carrie had refused to visit the hospital, afraid that her presence would reveal too much of her emotional turmoil.

'He has everything and everyone he needs,' she had

told Jay stubbornly. 'Our marriage is over, and as soon as I am able to do so I intend to leave.'

But she had not been able to allow herself to do so until she knew that Luc was well enough to leave hospital.

'Have they made the arrangements I requested?' she heard Luc questioning Jay as they reached her.

'Everything's organised,' Jay confirmed. 'There's no way, though, that you can give your speech from the square, Luc. Even the open balcony is out of the question. Instead, a loudspeaker system has been rigged up, and I've had new bulletproof glass installed around the balcony. It's real state-of-the-art stuff. If it's good enough for the American President then I guess you will be well protected by it. You can barely tell it's there, but let any old bullet try to get through it…'

'And just how many thousands of dollars has that cost?'

'Zillions,' Jay responded cheerfully. 'But it's my treat—a welcome home present.'

Luc was only inches from her now, his cool, grave gaze searching her face—no doubt looking for any weaknesses, Carrie decided.

She had her little speech all prepared, but it still took an effort for her to clear her throat and begin unemotionally.

'Thank you for what you did, Luc…for saving my life…'

She tensed as she saw the flicker of anger darkening his eyes.

'You're my wife,' he told her tersely. 'And—'

'The security guys are getting twitchy, Luc,' Jay intervened. 'Let's get inside…'

The minute they reached the private apartments Carrie stepped back, refusing to follow Luc into the salon.

He frowned and turned to look questioningly at her.

Amazingly, despite what he had been through, he looked as tough and strong as he had always done. In fact of the two of them she was the one who looked haggard and drawn, her body even thinner and her face paler, but of course she...

Abruptly she forced herself to concentrate on what she had to do.

'You and Jay have matters you need to discuss,' she announced crisply. 'Jay's told me about the public speech you want to make.' She swallowed.

At first when Jay had told her about Luc's public address she had cried out vehemently against it.

'What if someone else decides to try and kill him?' she had demanded emotionally. 'What does he think he's doing, taking that kind of risk?'

'That bullet wasn't intended for him, Carrie,' Jay had reminded her. 'And it wasn't intended to kill either. We know that the gunman simply wanted to make a point, to frighten you and draw attention to his cause. He hadn't allowed for the fact that Luc would see him and react in the way he did.'

'Maybe he didn't intend to kill, but that doesn't mean that someone even more dangerous might not try to,' Carrie had protested.

'Luc is insistent,' had been Jay's response. 'He says that—'

'It's his duty. Yes, I know,' Carrie had supplied bitterly.

'Carrie—' Luc began now, but Carrie shook her head quickly, her lips a mutely stubborn line, before turning on her heel to leave.

In her room everything was ready for her departure, and this time nothing was going to stop her.

Tomorrow Luc would make his speech to his people, no doubt assuring them that there was no need for them to be concerned, that he was fit and well again and that nothing and no one would ever stop him from fulfilling his responsibilities towards them—certainly not a misguided young man. A young man to whom, Carrie already knew, Luc was going to show the greatest of compassion and generosity in pardoning him for what he had done.

'Luc says that now all the disputed accounts have been closed there is no longer any reason for the genuine activists to continue with their protests. Interpol have already supplied him with the names of those they think might have infiltrated themselves into the group with an ulterior motive, and they are to be asked to leave the country or face up to the consequences of their actions which could well include incitement to regicide—theoretically still a treasonable offence here in S'Antander, and one that carries a life sentence of imprisonment,' Jay had told Carrie

Carrie was in her room, standing staring out of the window, when the door opened and Luc walked in. For a few seconds she was too shocked to speak. It was less than an hour since she had left him and she had assumed he would be tied up for many hours with matters of state.

'You still intend to leave, then,' he began without preamble.

Carrie nodded her head.

'Nothing has changed, Luc,' she told him stiffly. 'Everything I have already said to you still stands. Any relationship between us could only ever be sexual,' she announced curtly. 'You have no personal feelings for me, nor I for you.'

'Really? Yet Jay told me that when you first realised he had taken my place you thought he might have hurt me in some way.'

Carrie looked away from him.

'He told me that it was obvious how much you loved me!'

I *did*,' Carrie agreed woodenly, emphasising the past tense, but she could feel the raw pain of her unwanted emotions blocking her throat and anxiety began to take hold of her. She had to get away from Luc, and now…right now.

'And as for your claim that I have no personal feelings for you! How dare you say that, Carrie?' he demanded with soft anger. 'Haven't I shown you over and over again just how very; very powerful my love for you is? As a young man it was the hardest thing I ever did to let you go—'

'To let me go?' Carrie burst out. 'You didn't "let me go", Luc. You dismissed me from your life, and in the cruellest way—instructing your godmother to do your dirty work for you. Did you not know how much she would enjoy it?'

'What? I did no such thing! You were the one who *chose* to leave when my godmother approached you to warn you of the responsibility you would have to bear if our relationship continued and developed. You were the one who *chose* to walk away from it and from me. Of course I couldn't blame you. You were very young, with your whole life ahead of you, and if I had married you then, at eighteen, you would have been forced to change your whole life. I knew I had no right to ask you to make that kind of sacrifice.'

Carrie couldn't speak. She felt dizzy with the shock of his unwitting revelations.

'You…you blackmailed me into marrying you,' she managed to point out, 'and you didn't do that because you love me, Luc. You did it for political reasons; you told me that yourself. You even—'

'I am a man, and like all men I have my pride,' Luc told her fiercely. 'Of course I wasn't going to admit to you that from the first moment I looked out of my window and saw you in the square I knew—' He stopped. 'You have accused me of using the loss of our child in the most base and cruel of ways to gain my own ends. Have you any idea how hurtful I found that accusation? How offensive and unbelievable? Do you know why I allowed Maria to withdraw money from her trust fund when I didn't have to?'

Carrie stared mutely at him.

'I did it for you...because Harry is your brother and I wanted to do something that would please you. Had I chosen to I could have refused. If you don't believe me ask Maria yourself...and of course you will *not* believe me...'

The bitterness in his voice spiked Carrie's existing pain with guilt. She could see that Luc was speaking the truth, and she could see too that she had misjudged him. But he was still who he was. No, not *who* he was, she corrected herself sadly. He was *what* he was.

'These last weeks in hospital I've done a great deal of thinking, Carrie,' he told her quietly, 'and I've come to a decision. Tomorrow when I speak to my people I intend to announce my abdication!'

Carrie stared at him in shocked disbelief.

'I have done my best to fulfil my obligations to S'Antander, Carrie, and now I want "me" time—my time!' he told her fiercely. 'Now I want what other men take as their right. The woman I love in my arms, my bed...my life! The children I want to give her! The privacy and security to enjoy my life with her and them.'

'What are you trying to say? Luc, you can't do that— I won't let you!' Carrie protested wildly.

'You can't stop me,' Luc returned calmly. 'Wherever you go, Carrie, I am going too. Wherever that is. I shall follow you until you let me into your life, until you admit me back into your heart, until you let me prove to you how much I do love you.'

Carrie took a deep breath. He didn't mean it. He was just using emotional blackmail on her—just bluffing!

'Very well,' she told him coolly. 'If that is what you really want, Luc.' She walked towards the window and looked out for a few seconds before turning round and telling him, 'I've already booked my seat on a flight home tomorrow. I'm flying economy, of course…not private jet!'

'I mean what I'm saying, Carrie,' Luc told her steadily. 'Tomorrow morning I shall tell my people what I plan to do. I've already informed Jay, and I intend to inform my council this evening.'

Now he had really shocked her, but she refused to let him see it.

'You can't let Luc do this, Carrie.'

'Why not?' Carrie demanded as she faced Jay's accusing look across the width of her private sitting room.

Jay had walked in unannounced several minutes earlier, his face set and tense.

'You know why not,' he retorted grimly. 'S'Antander needs Luc, and if you let him walk away from this country it won't just be the country he's destroying—it will be a part of himself as well, and you know it. Think about it. Do you want to live with half the man all of the time, or have half of his time and all of the man?'

'That is moral blackmail, Jay,' Carrie pointed out sharply. 'And for your information I do not want Luc at all.'

'Liar!' Jay challenged her. 'You love him just as much as he does you. What is it with you?'

Carrie wouldn't make any response. Why should she? she asked herself stubbornly.

But later, when she was on her own, she couldn't stop thinking about what both Jay and Luc himself had said to her.

Luc did love her. And he loved her enough to give up his country for her!

'I've booked myself a seat to Heathrow on the day after tomorrow's flight. Once I get there...'

Carrie put down her cutlery and looked at Luc down the length of the formal dinner table.

'You might as well cancel it, Luc,' she told him levelly.

She could see the pain lance across his eyes before he hid it.

'Carrie, all I want is a chance to prove myself to you...myself and my love!'

The sensation, the emotion she had felt earlier when she had listened first to him and then to Jay returned, and this time she didn't try to fight against it. Some things were just meant to be, she acknowledged. Some things could not be avoided or denied. Some things, no matter how painful, simply had to happen. And for her this...Luc...was one of them. And not just one of them, but the most important of all, she admitted, as the icy remoteness encasing her heart melted in a sudden rush of warmth and love flowed back into it.

Luc loved her—she knew that now, just as surely as she knew that she loved him!

Lifting her chin, she told him firmly, 'I don't want you to abdicate, Luc.'

She could see him struggle to contain his anguish.

'There isn't really any point,' she added gently.

'There is every point,' Luc protested savagely. 'I want to be with you, Carrie—and more than that I *need* to be with you!'

Gravely Carrie looked at him. She could already feel the pressure, the burden of the weight of the choice she was being offered. How many times must Luc have felt that pressure, that burden, and how many times must he have forced himself to put aside his own needs and turn instead to carry the responsibility of his inheritance?

What was the measure…the test of true love, anyway? Demanding and getting a sacrifice? Or making the gift of one?

Just for a moment she allowed herself to gaze inwardly on her most private and precious dreams, and then very carefully she put them away and started to speak, as lightly as she could.

'As a little girl I always dreamed about being a princess, Luc, and I am not about to give up the chance to be one now just because you feel like being noble and making the ultimate sacrifice.'

Surprise, despair and just the merest beginnings of unsteady hope were all evident in Luc's eyes as he stared silently at her.

'Besides,' Carrie continued, 'what would our son say if he discovered I'd deprived him of the chance to play at soldiers and wear a uniform, never mind bedazzle any amount of pretty girls with his title?'

'Our son!'

Carrie heard the crash of the chair falling over as Luc stood up and pushed it out of the way in his hurry to get to her.

'Our son?' he repeated.

'Well, maybe not our son. Maybe our daughter,' Carrie

allowed, but the disjointed words were muffled against his chest and then smothered by his lips as he started to kiss her in a way that told her it would be a long, long time before she was going to be allowed to so much as breathe properly again, never mind speak!

EPILOGUE

'OH, GOODNESS, Carrie. He's so sweet—and just like Luc.'

Carrie laughed as Maria cooed enthusiastically over Carrie's six-week-old son, whose christening had been very much a public as well as a private affair.

His birth had been celebrated in S'Antander with enthusiastic delight. Carrie had become a much valued and loved public figure since her marriage, involving herself in several personal projects and charities, and Luc had encouraged her to do so.

'I never thought when Harry and I got married that you would be a mother before me—and especially not mother to Luc's son.' Maria grinned.

Maria's own baby was due at the end of the month, and Harry was hovering protectively at her side, anxious to get her safely back to England and the farm they had purchased, just in case all the excitement precipitated the birth.

Automatically Carrie glanced across the large state drawing room, looking for Luc. And, as though they were invisibly linked together, he raised his head at exactly the same time and looked back at her, causing the Euro diplomat who had been talking to him to follow the direction of his glance.

'Excuse me,' Luc apologised to the statesman. 'I must go and relieve my wife of her baby-carrying duties for a while.'

Things had certainly changed since he was a young

186

man, the statesman acknowledged, watching as Luc expertly scooped the sleeping baby out of his mother's arms and put him on his own shoulder.

'Luc. You're shocking all the old brigade.' Carrie laughed as she shook her head at him. 'That is not what they expect to see a "Serene Highness" do.'

'Well, then, they are just going to have to change their expectations,' Luc replied, giving her a warmly loving look. 'Because showing the world how important his wife and family are to this 'Serene Highness' is the most important thing to him. Which reminds me... How long is it, exactly, since I last told you I love you?'

Carrie pretended to consider.

'Oh...about an hour,' she teased him adoringly.

'As long as that? Well, tonight I promise I shall show you just how very much I do love you, in every single way,' Luc whispered softly to her.

And of course he did!

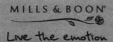

MILLS & BOON®

Live the emotion

Modern Romance™

SOLD TO THE SHEIKH by *Miranda Lee*

When supermodel Charmaine donates herself as a prize at a charity auction, she is amazed to discover the winning bidder is Prince Ali of Dubar, the same arrogant Arab sheikh she rejected a year ago! Her amazement turns to shock when Prince Ali makes her an outrageous offer...

HIS INHERITED BRIDE by *Jacqueline Baird*

Julia has rushed to Chile to see if an inheritance will give her the much needed money required to help her mother. But in order to claim a thing she must marry gorgeous Italian Randolfo Carducci! Multimillionaire Rand can give Julia anything she desires...but on *his* terms.

THE BEDROOM BARTER by *Sara Craven*

Chellie Greer is penniless and without her passport, stuck working in a seedy club with no means of escape. And then Ash Brennan walks in. What's such a powerful, irresistible stranger doing in a place like this? Ash offers her a way out – but Chellie has to wonder why...

THE SICILIAN SURRENDER by *Sandra Marton*

When it comes to women, rich and powerful Stefano Lucchesi has known them – except Fallon O'Connell. Beautiful and wealthy, she needs no one – least of all Stefano. Then an accident ends her career. Now she needs Stefano's help – even if that means surrender...

On sale 6th February 2004

Available at most branches of WHSmith, Tesco, Martins, Borders, Eason, Sainsbury's and all good paperback bookshops.

0104/01a

4 FREE

books and a surprise gift!

We would like to take this opportunity to thank you for reading this Mills & Boon® book by offering you the chance to take FOUR more specially selected titles from the Modern Romance™ series absolutely FREE! We're also making this offer to introduce you to the benefits of the Reader Service™—

- ★ FREE home delivery
- ★ FREE gifts and competitions
- ★ FREE monthly Newsletter
- ★ Exclusive Reader Service offers
- ★ Books available before they're in the shops

Accepting these FREE books and gift places you under no obligation to buy, you may cancel at any time, even after receiving your free shipment. Simply complete your details below and return the entire page to the address below. *You don't even need a stamp!*

YES! Please send me 4 free Modern Romance books and a surprise gift. I understand that unless you hear from me, I will receive 6 superb new titles every month for just £2.60 each, postage and packing free. I am under no obligation to purchase any books and may cancel my subscription at any time. The free books and gift will be mine to keep in any case.

P4ZED

Ms/Mrs/Miss/Mr ....Initials....................................
BLOCK CAPITALS PLEASE

Surname ....

Address ....

....

....Postcode..........................

Send this whole page to:
UK: FREEPOST CN81, Croydon, CR9 3WZ
EIRE: PO Box 4546, Kilcock, County Kildare (stamp required)